HEAT OF LOVE

Love on Madison Island 2

MEKA JAMES

For all the readers with firefighter fantasies.

To all the women over 40 who are not invisible, and who are nowhere near past their "prime".

Thanks to the Wordmakers and Lily who believe in my writing even when I don't. And an extra special shout out to Coralie who always has a shoulder available to cry on and extra words of encouragement to keep me motivated.

Cover design by Kylie Sek of Cover Culture
Illustration by Tamara Davies
Edited by: Tera Cuskaden

<u>Love On Madison Island</u>

Renovation of Love

Heat of Love

Mechanics of Love

Follow me on Bookbub for up-to date information about future releases

❋ I ❋

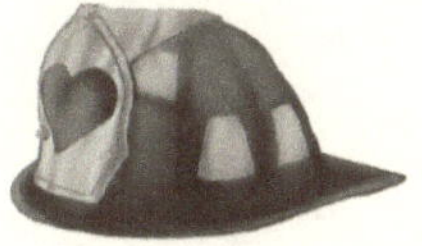

REGINA

IT WAS A SURREAL FEELING TO WITNESS EVERYTHING YOU'D worked for, everything your family had built over four generations, be taken from you. Even from across the street, the heat from the flames warmed my skin. I'd never understood what people meant when they'd say they had an out of body experience, but that had to be what I was having. None of it seemed real. It *couldn't* be real.

People were shouting. Sirens blared. A crackle and hiss as more flames sparked and lit up the night sky like a cruel fireworks display. Somewhere that sounded both far off and extremely close a person screamed and cried out in disbelief.

This wasn't happening.

This wasn't happening.

There was pressure on my hand. Other voices were trying to cut through the cries.

"Regina!"

"Regina!"

My name, someone was calling my name. I turned and saw Cynthia running toward me. More pressure crushing my fingers. It was Momma. She was crying into Daddy's shoulder while holding onto me for dear life.

Cynthia threw her arms around my shoulders. "Oh god, Regina. What happened?"

She put her palms on my cheeks. They were cold. So cold in comparison to how hot it was. Shouting. So much shouting and questions—too many questions. I opened my mouth to speak, to answer the unanswerable, but no words came. A long, soul-shattering scream ripped from my throat as reality sank in.

It was gone.

❧

I OPENED my eyes and quickly closed them again against the bright sunlight. I was home, in my bed. *How did I get home?* There was movement beside me, and I looked over to find Cynthia curled up and sleeping peacefully. Last time I'd woken to find her sleeping beside me had been after the accident.

Once again, my lids fluttered shut as last night's events replayed in my head. I tried to take in a breath but couldn't fully inflate my lungs.

It was gone.

Emptiness spread through me as pain squeezed my heart. I swung my legs over the side and pushed into a sitting position. Cynthia startled at the movement.

"Hey. You okay? You need something?" Her voice was groggy with sleep, but she was up and beside me, rubbing her eyes.

I could only shake my head, and I willed the tears burning the back of my eyes to stay put. They didn't listen.

She wrapped her arms around my shoulders and held me tight, rocking us gently. "It's going to be okay. It will all be okay."

"How did this happen?"

"I don't know, but we'll figure it out and then we'll rebuild."

I sat up and wiped the tears from my cheeks. "Thanks for being here."

"Not a single thanks needed. You go shower and I'll get breakfast started if Marcel hasn't."

I frowned. "Marcel?"

"Yeah, he slept in Darnell's room, and your parents are in the guest room."

I massaged at my temples, hoping to stave off the quickly building headache. More flashes from last night of Momma crying, Daddy trying to console her. How did this happen on my watch? I was sure Big Momma and Nana were rolling over in their graves knowing what I let happen to their pride and joy.

"How is Momma? The stress is not good for either of them."

Cynthia nodded. "She was concerned about you. We all were."

I let out a heavy sigh. "It doesn't seem real, you know?"

"I know. I texted Irene. She'll probably call later today. She was going to see if she could rearrange her patients, but if not, she'll be here Saturday. And your daddy got in touch with Darnell, who was ready to drive home last night. So, expect to see him soon."

Mention of my baby boy—who was now more a man— brought a smile to my face. Though I'd mostly adjusted to being an empty-nester, I still looked forward to his visits. However, this was not a reason I'd want him coming to see me.

I rolled my shoulders in a failed attempt to release some tension and glanced at the clock. Unease made my stomach ache. I should have been heading to the bakery, preparing for the day. Instead, I sat with my friend, who rubbed small circles on my back, and an absolute loss of purpose covered me like a wet, scratchy blanket.

"I'm going to shower, then I need to go...I need to see."

"Okay. We'll go with you."

I squeezed her hand as emotion clogged my throat. There was zero use in arguing with her over her need to not babysit me. My friend had already seen me at my worst sixteen years ago. With her and Irene I didn't have to worry about being strong and pulled together all the time. I pushed off the bed and shuffled over to my bathroom.

As the water heated up, I rested my palms on the granite countertop and stared at my reflection. The bags under my bloodshot eyes seemed to be packed for a month-long trip. I'd survived the loss of my husband and the near loss of my son.

"This will not beat me," I hissed to my reflection.

And it would not. My heart ached and my soul was crushed, but this would not beat me. I'd always handled my business, and this would be no different.

After my shower, I went through my usual routine, including my makeup. I may have had nowhere to go, but I needed some normalcy. Something to help remind myself of my new mantra: this would not beat me.

Voices carried down the hall, reminding me I wouldn't have to deal with the situation alone. The scent of coffee and sausage made my stomach growl.

Dad spotted me first. "Morning, sweetheart." He walked over, hugged me tight, and kissed my cheek.

He ushered me over to the table where Cynthia and Marcel sat. Momma put a plate in front of me and patted my arm before she gathered the empty dishes.

"Has anyone seen my phone?" I asked after taking a bite of eggs.

There were calls to make, and I needed to talk to the insurance company. Rebuilding couldn't get underway until they paid out, and I knew the red tape would be a bitch. Same as when I'd had to deal with the bullshit from the life insurance people.

"It might still be in the car," Marcel answered. He pushed back from the table, kissed my friend on the top of her head, and then went outside.

I grinned at her. "Have I told you lately how glad I am you came to your senses."

She rolled her eyes. "Really. This is what you want to bring up?"

I shrugged. "Momma agrees with me."

On cue, Mom chimed in. "Yes, you snatched Madison's most eligible bachelor."

"What am I? Chopped liver?" Dad asked, incredulous tone coloring each word.

"Man, please. You ain't been a bachelor since the Stone Age." She walked up behind him and wrapped her arms around his neck. "Just the way I like it."

He turned and gave her a quick kiss. "Damn right."

This was perfect. A tiny bubble of normal that could almost make me forget. Almost.

Marcel returned, his son in tow, and set my dead cellphone next to my plate. MJ greeted us and offered his sympathies. He also assured me they'd be ready and waiting to get the reconstruction underway soon as they had the green light. He and his father said their goodbyes, and Cynthia excused herself to go get ready.

Momma sat beside me and wrapped her arms around my shoulders. "I can tell you're blamin' yourself."

"How can I not? First all that crap with Trent, and now a fire." Just speaking that man's name made my blood pressure spike.

I still had a hard time wrapping my head around the fact a man we'd trusted, that I'd trusted, had stolen from me. I'd considered him more than an employee; he'd been a friend. Or so I'd believed. I'd listened, and caved on not doing it all on my own. Gave him more responsibility, and he'd returned that kindness by forging orders and skimming off the top. Right under my nose. How could I not feel inept? Not only did I not catch it sooner, but I hadn't even suspected it in the first place. Things were just starting to settle from that and his arrest, and now my bakery had caught fire.

"Don't let that thievin', lyin' bastard take up your energy," Dad spat.

He was mostly removed from the business other than to offer support and encouragement. And be first in line as a taste tester for new recipes. But that didn't mean he stayed out of the loop. He may have been a retired postal worker, but the bakery was a family business.

"Exactly what your father said. And as for the fire, we can't predict these things. It might have been some faulty gas line, or dry lightning. We just can't say. Either way, it's out of your control."

I knew they were right, but that didn't stop the self-deprecating thoughts. I was at the helm and needed to protect it until I was ready to retire and hand the reins over to my niece Tricia. We would rebuild, and the legacy would continue. I didn't care what it took.

"Cynthia is going to go with me to the bakery, then we'll pop over to the fire station to see if Chief Morris can give me some info. I'm gonna need it for the insurance, I'm guessin', and the sooner we know the sooner we can file our claim and get back at it."

"Do you want us to come?" Dad asked. "You know Pat and I are fishing buddies."

"I know, Daddy. But I'm a big girl and I can handle it."

"You sure? Not that I don't think he'd be straight with you, but you know how men are," Momma said.

"I feel like I should take some offense here," Dad grumbled, shifting back and forth in his seat.

Mom waved him off. "Oh please."

"Ready when you are," Cynthia announced on her return.

"I got it, Daddy. But if I think he's giving me the run around, I'll let you ride in and save me." I gave them both kisses. "Lock up when you leave."

❧   2   ❧

ALEC

YELLOW CAUTION TAPE SURROUNDED THE BURNED-OUT building. Soot discolored the white brick façade. The front windows were shattered, but the sidewalk was clear of any broken shards. Just A Bit of Sugar was a fun play on words considering the type of business. The decorative sign seemed to be the only thing untouched by the flames and water.

When I'd gotten the call early in the morning that a smaller department had requested an investigator, I'd half expected it to be a case of local teens bored and setting brush fires. Accepting the job in Savannah meant I wouldn't be in a place where I'd see a lot of action as an investigator since it was one of the smaller regions. Hell, in the six months I'd been part of the Savannah Fire Department, the station only had gotten four fire-related calls. Well, serious fire-related calls.

My mom had been happy about the move since it meant I would be less on the frontlines. Although she and Dad supported my career choice, she'd rather see me behind a desk away from the danger. I wanted to be an investigator for the better pay, but that didn't mean I didn't love the rush of running into a building. Man against nature—there was nothing more exhilarating.

Most of my area consisted of smaller surrounding cities that only had a volunteer department. Being sent out to one of those wasn't a scenario I'd expected to face often. Or ever, if I were being honest. How ironic that my first call was for just that reason. Madison Island, a town I hadn't even known existed, small or quaint as my mother would call it. I saw it more as boredom and a slow death.

An older man who looked like he could double as a Black Santa, white beard and hair and the belly required for the job, walked toward me. "You must be the investigator, I'm Chief Morris."

"That'd be me, sir. Alec Hodge, at your service."

"Good, good. Glad you got here so quick. It's a damn shame. I know the family and this place...the whole town is feeling the loss."

The old-timer smacked his lips and shook his head. I shuddered at the thought of living in a place like this full time. Hell, I was surprised I hadn't gone completely stir-crazy in Savannah. I missed the hustle and bustle of Atlanta. Nightclubs, bars, a variety of women. One-nighters were much easier in the city, though if there had been one perk to my move, it would be that living farther away made separation from possible clingy encounters a breeze. Been there. Done that. But I still needed out. I'd given myself two years tops at the smaller department for the experience, which would make me a much more attractive candidate for one of the bigger areas. I needed fires to make that happen, and a fire I had, which gave me the chance to show my expertise. A twinge of guilt hit the back of my mind; some poor soul had clearly lost their business, and I was focusing on what a real case would do for my career goals.

"So, Chief, what made you call me in?"

He scratched at his full beard. "Welp, in all my years here, I ain't quite dealt with nothing like this. A random kitchen fire here or there, but this..." He gestured at the building. "Something ain't right with what happened. I'm semi-retired, got just a couple guys that rotate at the station. Not equipped for the likes of this."

The man sucked his teeth while giving the destroyed space a long look. He suspected possible arson? Interesting.

I ducked beneath the caution tape, and broken glass crunched under my boots as I entered the wreckage. The scent of charred wood and burnt plastic filled my nostrils. The front room didn't have damage to the point I couldn't tell what the place once was. Tables and chairs were overturned, the large glass display case had a crack down the center. A chalkboard sign half erased by the water dangled sideways from one chain listed food items and prices. My quick cursory glance didn't detect a flashpoint, which told me the fire hadn't started in this area.

Under different circumstances, the bakery probably was a welcoming place to grab a coffee and donut. I snapped pictures and kept focus in search of a flashpoint. If this was arson, the business owner was always the top suspect.

"A damn shame I tell ya. They'd just done some remodeling a few years back."

I glanced over my shoulder at the chief and made a mental note. Maybe the owner was over-extended. The burnt odor grew stronger as I rounded the counter and headed to the back. The room, which I suspected at one time was white and clean, now sported walls burned down to the studs around the backdoor.

Metal tables with legs buckled from the heat. The floor was a sticky mess of flour and maybe sugar, as the bags that were once probably stacked on the overturned racks were busted and scattered everywhere. On the far side of the room was a walk-in cooler, and the door seemed to be holding. The same couldn't be said for the fridges that lined the wall closest to the back entry. The level of damage there meant it was probably where things burned hotter because it was the ignition point.

I strolled to that area for closer inspection. "Has the owner been having financial troubles?" As I kneeled next to the door, the scent of gasoline hit my nostrils, and I noted what looked like a V pattern that was singed around the edges on the linoleum floor. It was possible someone had stood outside pouring the liquid at the base.

"Regina? Nah. Folks love her. Hell, my morning wasn't the same without her deep roast coffee and a bear claw."

"Business was good then?"

Before he could answer, female voices got our attention. Someone tugged on the warped back door, then the suggestion was made to go around front. Who would be trying to break in, in the middle of the day? It wasn't uncommon for people to scavenge around fire sites, there was always something people could find to sell, or in cases like a business, some hoped they would possibly find money.

We arrived at the front just in time to see two women ducking under the tape.

"Excuse me, but you can't be in here," I called out in an attempt to stop them from entering further.

"The hell I can't," shot back the shorter of the two.

I opened my mouth to speak when the chief moved around me, arms open wide.

"Regina. How are you holding up?"

She was the owner? I didn't know why but I was expecting someone older, more grandmotherly with the way the chief had talked about knowing the family and hinting at how long the place had been around. Instead, I was faced with a woman who had curves for days. The jeans she wore showed off her voluptuous figure. Full hips and thick thighs just how I liked them. Her purple V-neck T-shirt did nothing to tone down an extremely large pair of breasts.

"I know they're impressive, but you look old enough to have seen titties before, so eyes up, fella."

Both the chief and the woman she'd entered with laughed. I had no shame in appreciating an attractive woman. It was a favorite pastime of mine, but doing so on the job and with the owner who might have burned down her own property probably wasn't the best time.

I smiled and stuck my hand out. "Alec Hodge. Your chief called me in."

She glanced at my extended appendage for about half a second before she took it. "Regina Parker. And that's my friend Cynthia Lewis." The other woman with short gray hair and a friendly smile waved. "And called you in for what exactly?"

"He's a special fire investigator up from Savannah." The chief spoke up.

She stepped back, planted her hands on her hips, and pushed her purple-tinted lips into a pout while she eyed me up and down. "What are you investigating? Other than the girls, that is?" She was blunt and pulled no punches. I could respect that.

But she was also more lively and not weepy for someone who'd just lost their business less than twelve hours ago. She was pulled together, complete with her face perfectly made and her red dreadlocks twisted in an up-do.

I spread my arms wide. "This, Mrs. Parker. Your chief doesn't think the fire was accidental."

She arched one perfectly groomed brow. "It's Miss, but just call me Regina. You young, but not that young." Again she gave me a once-over, then turned her attention to the chief.

He put his hands up. "Just a precaution. I was gonna call Albert later and talk with y'all."

Cynthia wrinkled her brow and her gaze darted from the chief, to me, and back to the chief again. "But you think it was intentional?"

Chief Morris rubbed the back of his neck. "I don't rightly know, which is why I called in Alec over here. Besides, your insurance company will probably want some sort of report for the claim. Better if it comes from someone extra official."

Regina sighed, and for the first time since the interaction started, weariness blanketed her features. She turned her whiskey-colored eyes in my direction. "So?"

"So...what?"

"Was it an accident or not?"

"Not sure. We were just getting started when you and your partner in crime illegally crossed the tape." I glanced over at Cynthia, who smiled and shook her head.

"Boy, please. It says caution, not keep out. My building, so I can be here."

Her hair color certainly matched her spirited attitude. I swallowed back a retort to her second dig at my age. Being combative with Ms. Regina Parker would do me no good. She didn't seem like the kind of woman who took too well to someone trying to assert authority, even if they had a reason. If I had to deal with her often while I was here, my time in Mayberry would be way more exciting than I thought.

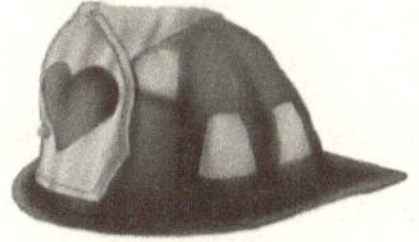

REGINA

THE "SPECIAL" INVESTIGATOR GRINNED AT ME. IT WAS ONE OF those "I look good, and I know you know it" grins. The type that got women to drop their drawers and throw all logical thought to the wind. The kind of lopsided, dimple revealing, pearly whites on full display grin that could turn me into that woman. He was a young buck, and under different circumstances I wouldn't mind taking him for a spin.

"For your safety and until I'm done investigating, this is me politely asking you to stay out of *your* building."

I clucked my tongue and rolled my eyes. "Fine. I can accommodate your request, but after I go to the office."

"How about you tell me what you need, and I'll get it. It is dangerous, plus I would like you not to disturb too much."

This man was testing my already shot patience. Though dealing with his somewhat arrogant good-looking self kept me from breaking down into tears again. Standing in my bakery with the foul odor of burned wood and melted plastic filling my nostrils instead of coffee and sugar made it hard to breathe. I'd tried to ignore the crunch beneath my feet and the utter disarray of my usually organized shop. Everything was dark and dirty and not right. The weight that'd been on my chest since I'd opened my eyes got heavier. It was ruined. All ruined. And if Chief Morris thought it wasn't accidental... I didn't even know how to process that information.

I shook my head and focused on the task at hand. "How about you accompany me. And you can investigate my backside as closely as you did my front. I need to get into the safe, and you may be cute and all, but I'm not about to give you my combination."

Chief Morris tried to cover his laugh with a cough and Cynthia simply smiled and muttered a low, "Well then."

The man standing directly in front of me pressed his lips together and nodded his head slowly. "Deal. I am here to get to the bottom of things, and I need to make sure I do a thorough job." A smirk lifted the corner of his mouth.

Chief Morris cleared his throat. "That might be our cue to leave." He extended his arm and ushered Cynthia out the front door.

I eyed Special Investigator Hodge up and down before strutting toward the back with him on my heels. Pushing through the double steel doors I had to steady myself as I surveyed more of the damage up-close-and-personal for the first time. I'd known it would be bad, but seeing it with my own eyes made my chest constrict and my eyes burn. Everything was a mess. The floor was a white sludge mixture, the walls were black. And with each move, water sloshed under our feet, echoing in my ears reminding me again that it was gone. Generations of work stolen, burned in a flash.

I tried to take in a breath but couldn't stand the foul air. The stench seared my senses. This was no accident. At least that's what the chief suspected, and which was why tall, dark, and extremely sexy was trailing behind me. I didn't think anything could be salvaged. The tables were warped. My large side-by-side refrigerator doors were buckled. Everything was ruined. I carefully stepped over the debris trying not to disturb too much, but each crunch or splash was another arrow to my already bleeding soul.

"What do you need from the safe?" Alec inquired.

"The deposits. Normally I would take them to the bank in the morning after we'd opened while my old manager..." I didn't bother with the rest of that statement, I didn't need to let my mind wander back to Trent right now.

"So, your money from yesterday has been unsecured this entire time?"

"I mean yeah. It's not like it was sitting out in the open. I do have a safe, and this is how I've always done it. The bank is closed by the time we shut down at night. Besides, no one in this town would steal from me."

The moment those words flew out of my mouth my throat closed up at the lie that had just tumbled free. Though, in my defense it used to not always be a lie, but Trent changed that. It was a knife to my heart and my back.

My office wasn't spared from the destruction. It wasn't as bad as the kitchen, but still, there were singed papers, water damage, and the computer was shot. I was thankful I'd kept yesterday's receipts along with the cash in the safe so that wasn't a loss. And we had a backup system for tracking orders and supplies at an off-site server. I wouldn't be set back too much. Small victories to celebrate.

"How long have you owned this place?" he asked, leaning against the doorframe.

"The bakery has been in my family for four generations. My great-grandmother started it, then my grandmother, followed by my mother, and now I helm the ship. When my time is up, my niece is poised to take over."

"A family business then?"

"Yup. Most folks around here start their days by walking through these doors." I kept my back to him as I pushed in the combination. I didn't need to let the stranger see how much being in this place was hurting me.

I could tell his eyes were boring into me. He seemed to be watching my every move since I'd arrived, and it was only partially due to his appreciation of my tits. *Does he think I did this?* If so, he was out of his damn mind. I loved my place. It was my life.

"How long will your investigation take?"

"It depends."

With the locked blue money bag safely under my armpit I turned to face him. "On?"

Again, he stared at me, this time not just on the girls, but at me.

"On how cooperative everyone is as I try to figure out the cause of the fire."

I tilted my chin up. "Well, either you want to jump my bones right here and now in the middle of this mess, or you're looking at me like I'm suspect number one. Which one is it?"

"Are you always this forward?"

"Yes. Life is too short, and I am too damn old to be beating around the fucking bush. If I want to know something I ask."

He grinned, and again I was sure that smile had gotten him out of a lot of trouble. Or maybe into some. The goatee surrounding those full lips drew my attention. The neatly trimmed beard, waves in his hair I was sure he spent hours brushing to make look absolutely perfect...a well-groomed man was just my type. Even dressed in an outfit that probably wasn't flattering on a lot of men, he made the plain blue T-shirt with the SFD emblem on the right side of his chest, and the equally utilitarian black cargo pants and military-style boots work for him.

"It's too early to rule out anyone, Ms. Parker. Like I said, the chief and I were just getting started when you stopped by."

I wouldn't let his statement get to me. He was just doing his job, something I understood. People did crazy shit sometimes, but I enjoyed too many luxuries in life to fuck around with something like insurance fraud that would land my ass in jail. No thank you.

"Are you staying in town while you do your investigating, or are you driving back and forth to Savannah every day?"

He tilted his head slightly. "Is that important?"

I shrugged. "Not really. My only thing is the quicker you figure out what happened here, the sooner I can get on with rebuilding and get my business back up and running. Time is money."

"Understood. And where can I find you if I have more questions?"

I glanced around my disaster of a desk and found the little holder with business cards in it. Luckily the ones in the middle were semi dry enough to serve their purpose.

"Got a pen?"

He pulled the one clipped to the side of his pocket and handed it to me. I flipped my card over and scribbled my number on the back. "Here you go. This way you can reach me whenever you need some cooperation. But, if you wanted my number, all you had to do was ask. No need to keep up pretenses."

Flirting with this man wasn't really doing me any favors, but it kept my mind off the wreckage around me. I could focus on him and not on my livelihood literally up in smoke.

4

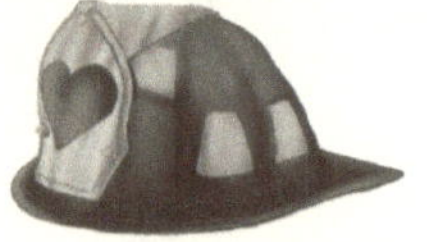

ALEC

As I followed Chief Morris to the firehouse my thoughts went back to the feisty bakery owner *Miss* Regina Parker. She certainly wasn't what I'd expected, and I certainly wasn't expecting the low-key flirting she seemed to be doing with me. However, I was here to work and not get caught up with a quickie fling with the woman I was investigating. But that didn't mean the business card with her phone number wasn't burning a hole in my pocket.

Chief Morris pulled into the empty bay, and I parked the department truck in a space next to a little compact. The red brick building was about what I would have expected for a small department in this town. One engine and a couple guys hanging about, who greeted the chief as he exited the vehicle.

Regina had been correct; staying close by made more sense than driving the forty minutes to and from Savannah until this was wrapped up. The chief offered up the bunkhouse at the station, giving me the room reserved for him because he was too old to sleep on a crappy twin bed. I understood that. I hated sleeping on those damn beds, too. But comfort wasn't the point; functionality was.

The chief decided to show me around so I would know my

way. Not like I could get lost in Madison. It felt like the entire town was one giant square, but I wouldn't shit on his hospitality.

I smiled and nodded at the guys sitting around before following him into the building.

The chief hooked his thumbs in the belt loops of his jeans and rocked back on his heels. "Welp, this is it. Not fancy, but space to lay your head without having to make that drive. One or two of the guys are always here. They know you'll be staying, and they'll accommodate you whatever you need."

"Much appreciated, Chief."

"No, thank you for coming. Still hurts my soul to see what happened, but we'll get it fixed right as rain and they'll be back in business in no time." He patted me on the shoulder and shook his head before he exited the room.

I had to admit this was a step up from the digs in Savannah, where I had to sleep in the bunkhouse with the rest of the firefighters. The only person who got special privileges and their own private quarters was the chief there. I'd hoped the promotion would come with my own room, but the department was too small for that even though it was bigger than the place I was in currently. It wasn't that I didn't like the team at the station, but when you hit a certain age, living like you're in a dormitory even though it was for your job got real old real fucking quick.

In the corner of the room was a small desk with a chair. I dropped my laptop bag on top and pulled the silver device free. At least I could get a little bit of work done, upload the pictures I'd taken, and start writing up my preliminary reports.

It was definitely arson, but I still needed more information before making a complete determination. Regina was adamant she had nothing to do with it. And my gut was inclined to believe her. The chief made it out as if the entire town revered the woman, so if not her, then who? And why? I shoved my hand into my pocket and closed my fingers around the business card, smiling.

I knew exactly where I would get those answers.

I RUBBED at the stiffness in my neck trying to work out the kinks from sleeping on what had to be the world's most uncomfortable bed and stone like pillow ever. Two nights on it was two too many. If I was going to be here any longer, I was going to need to find a store to at the very least replace that fucking pillow because there was no way in hell I could get any sleep with the current one. As I approached the bakery, I noticed a line of people wrapping around the building.

"What the fuck? Do the people around here not think?" This was an active site. Why did it look like some sort of tourist destination?

Luckily, a car was leaving, and I was able to snag a parking spot right in front of the burned-out location. I threw my truck into park and took a few deep breaths, trying to figure out what the hell was going on and what the fuck these people were doing. I followed the line of patrons to the back parking lot, and there was none other than Miss Regina Parker in the brightest scrubs I'd ever laid eyes on—that surprisingly matched her lip color— laughing, talking, and working.

I cussed under my breath. I'd told that woman to stay out of the building, yet here she was, peddling her baked goods. I weaved my way to the makeshift counter where she stood next to an older woman with a striking resemblance to her.

When Regina saw me approach, she flashed me the biggest smile ever. "Well, good morning, Special Investigator Hodge. Can I get you anything?"

She took money and handed off a lime-green box to the customer in front of her. They nodded in my direction.

"Can I talk to you for a second?"

She spread her hands out in front of her. "As you can see, I'm more than a little busy."

The older woman looked me up and down and a sly smile pulled at her lips. "It's okay, Gina. Trish and I can handle this.

You go talk to whoever this fine hunk of man is." She winked at me. Which shouldn't have amused me as much as it did.

"Momma, don't go gettin' no ideas."

Mom? That was her mom? I glanced back at the older woman, and I could see the resemblance. Lighter complexion, but the same wide mouth and playful eyes. Unlike her daughter, this woman's hair was salt and pepper, secured with a scarf knotted at the top of her head but had spiral curls framing her face. Which had surprisingly few wrinkles. Good genes in the family ran deep. Regina came from behind the table and followed me off to a far corner of the lot away from her crowd of customers, one which was the very fire chief I had seen two days before.

"Can I ask you what the hell you're doing?"

She planted her hands on her hips and jutted her chin up. "I'm sorry, but who the fuck are you to question me, Special Investigator? You need to watch your tone and don't be addressing me like I'm some youngin' with her nose wide open and can be talked to any which way."

I closed my eyes and took in a breath. She was right. I was out of line in how I addressed her. "My apologies, Ms. Parker. Let's try this again. I asked you not to go inside the building, yet here you are set up shop, hosting a bake sale in the parking lot while I'm still investigating the scene."

"It's called working, Special Investigator. And do you think I'm dense?"

I held my tongue on my immediate response and pinched the bridge of my nose. "No, ma'am, I don't think that. But I do have to question what the hell it is you're doing right now."

She huffed and straightened her shoulders, pushing those very distracting breasts upward.

"You said don't go inside. I didn't. You didn't say a damn thing about not being on the property. The people in this town look for their donuts and scones and apple fritters and their fucking coffee, and I'm going to give it to them. Even if that means I'm selling it in the back parking lot of my burned-out building."

I massaged my temples. The pain from my neck radiated up into my skull and rattled around like a ping pong ball.

"I need to work, Special Investigator Hodge. And my people need to work. I have employees that depend on their paychecks. You can't expect me to just sit around twiddling my damn thumbs. That's not how I do things. So, you go investigate and do your job, and you let me do mine."

She didn't even wait for a response before she turned on her heel and sashayed away, the swing of her hips maybe purposely more pronounced than normal, but I couldn't be sure. What I did know was she was going to make this whole situation way more stressful if I was going to have to come here every day and fight through a crowd of people trying to get their pastries before they went to work.

Realizing it was a losing battle, I shook my head and decided not to fight it, because short of tying her up somewhere, I didn't think there was any way to keep her away from the place. But her unorthodox actions cleared her as a suspect. What woman would burn down her own building only to be here two days later and picking up where she left off?

And from the looks of things with the line of people, the community wanted her much as she wanted them. As I turned to head inside, she was walking back toward me, swinging her hips and a cup in her hand.

"This one's on the house, Special Investigator."

"You know you can just call me Alec, right?"

She lifted one shoulder. "What would be the fun in that?"

I took the lid off the cup and inhaled the heavenly scent. That alone was better than the sludge that came out of the machine at the firehouse. "Is this a bribe, Miss Parker?"

A coy smile graced her orange-tinged lips. "Baby, if I was going to bribe you, it sure as hell wouldn't be with coffee."

I licked my lips before taking a sip of the sweetened black liquid. "I'll be sure to keep that in mind."

She walked away for the second time, with the chief making his way over to me.

"You can't keep a good woman down, that's for damn sure," he said, taking a bite of a large confectionery dessert.

"Is that the bear claw you were talking about?" I had to admit, the damn thing looked delicious.

"Yep. I don't know how she did it, but she somehow managed to make all the favorites and transfer them over here and was ready and waiting to serve us all."

"How did y'all even know she would be here? Is there some sort of secret network for pastries wanted in this town?"

The chief laughed. "Not quite, but it is a small place and word gets around easy. Plus, we're a community, and if coming here and buying a cup of coffee or bear claw will help her get back up and running faster, then that's what we're gonna do."

I could respect that. That's how small towns were. Or so I heard. I'd barely talked to my neighbors at my old complex. And the lady on the other side of my duplex? Well, she'd smile and be friendly, and I was always polite. But there'd be no entanglements with the new neighbor. At least not this time. I'd learned that lesson the hard way. Having what I thought was just sex with someone who lived close when she thought it was a budding relationship had been a disaster. And drama I would not repeat.

5

REGINA

I WAS BONE TIRED BY THE TIME WE SOLD OUT OF THE PASTRIES I had managed to make. I was thankful for the help of my staff, my parents, and Cynthia and Marcel for loaning out their ovens and their time so that I could get this pop-up store up and running. It wasn't ideal, but it was better than nothing. Even if Alec had been annoyed at the idea of me handling my business. Which I was sure was a major fucking overstep of his duties.

I honestly didn't think it would work out. I had serious doubts, but I also knew I couldn't sit around and do nothing for Lord knew how fucking long while he investigated. I didn't even know what he had left to determine. Yes, it was arson, and that truth hurt my soul. Who would purposely burn down my bakery? It made no sense.

My mind kept racing at the thought of someone doing this deliberately. I wanted to think it was just random. I didn't want to speak out loud that the only person who would do something like this was Trent. Though I hoped I was wrong. I hoped he wouldn't sink to that level, but he had stolen from me, and he hadn't taken too kindly to being fired. Or arrested. I'd "ruined" his life, he'd cried. Anger flashed hot and fast as I recalled that statement. He had some damn gall, that was for sure.

Still, I hadn't spoken my suspicions out loud, but I could tell those close to me were thinking the same thing. He was the only one that had any reason to do something so terrible. At the same time, it made no sense. He was already facing legal action from the theft. Arson would be putting the final nail in his coffin.

"Mom, is that everything?" Darnell asked after sliding the last table in the back of Marcel's truck. He'd happily loaned it to us because my little SUV wouldn't hold everything. Though I suspected his wife's skills of "persuasion" helped in that decision.

I headed over to my boy, happy to have him here with me, and hugged him tight even though he complained about the public display of affection. He humored me, and he only half pretended he didn't like it, but deep in his heart, we both knew he was nothing but a mama's boy. The older he'd gotten, the more he'd grown to be damn near the spitting image of his father, from the dark complexion to the black, low cut curls on his head. But he had my eyes, so it wasn't a total wash.

"Yeah, I think that's it. How did it feel to work at the bakery again? You hadn't done that since you were like sixteen."

"Crazy, that's for damn sure. I wasn't expecting such a big turnout, but I'm glad they came out here to support you, Momma."

"Me too, baby, me too."

The man who was the current obstacle appeared out of the back door. Our eyes met, and he gave me a little wave.

"Momma, you ready to go? I need to hit the road since I do have to get back to work tomorrow."

"Yeah, give me a sec. I'll be right there."

I strolled over to Special Investigator Hodge, who was busy jotting down more information into a notebook. Dressed in another well-fitting T-shirt and relaxed fit jeans that were tight enough to show off what I imagined to be muscular thighs and a firm ass. Living in the same town your whole life leaves the man candy perks in a sad state. His presence, though for a terrible reason, at least had an upside.

"Are you just about done?"

"Yes, I think I am. I have most of the information I need. Just a few loose ends, then I should be all wrapped up."

"So, what does that mean?"

"It means I'll be out of your hair, and the police or whoever would take over from there. I don't track down the arsonist. I only determine if there was one. And how they started it."

Again, my heart clinched at the thought of someone deliberately doing this to me. Part of the reason I was able to pull off the pop-up store was because I'd spent most of the night tossing and turning. I figured if I wasn't going to get a decent night's sleep at least I could make my ass productive. Special Investigator didn't need to know that I had snuck inside just to get my boxes. Most had been waterlogged, but I had a case that I was able to salvage. Wiping out the grocery store shelves of flour, sugar, and all the other items I needed was one thing, but those boxes, I had to have them.

Someone had deliberately taken from me and my family. But I pushed the thoughts aside. I couldn't dwell; I could only move forward. "Does that mean you'll be leaving soon?"

He folded his arms across his broad chest and rolled his tongue along his bottom lip. "Yeah. Probably a day or so."

Damn, there went my eye candy. "Maybe I should offer you another non-bribe."

His troublemaking smirk appeared and put his deep dimples on display. He gave me another appreciative glance, his eyes not just lingering on the girls this time. "What exactly did you have in mind, Miss Parker?"

"Well, I was talkin' dinner. But the way you eyeballing me, I'm thinkin' you want dessert."

He stepped closer to me, so much I could feel the heat radiating off his body. He smelled of stale smoke from being inside the building, but underneath that was a hint of sweetness. A mixture of tobacco and clove.

"Just a bit of sugar, right? I mean if that's what you're known for, I figure I should have a taste before I leave."

He was bold, that was for damn sure. I took the pen and notebook from his hand and scribbled my address at the top of a blank page. "Seven o'clock, Special Investigator."

"With bells on, Miss Parker."

Darnell frowned as I got to the truck. "What was that all about?"

"Nothing. I was simply extending a little hospitality."

He shook his head. "I don't even want to begin to know what that's code for."

"Boy, please. I offered to make him dinner because he's here and probably eating crap food around the firehouse."

He cranked up the truck. "Uh-huh. Yeah sure. Both y'all's body language said dinner. Good thing I'm heading out today."

I rolled my eyes. "Maybe you should take a few less psychology classes."

While I knew my son realized his mom was probably not living the life of a spinster, he also knew or rather maybe didn't want to acknowledge that I did have companionship from time to time.

My focus had been on raising him and growing the business after we'd lost his father. But a woman had needs. Discreet needs, but needs all the same. Mr. Alec Hodge could be perfect for scratching my long-standing itch as of late.

❧

"I CAN'T BELIEVE you're flirting with that firefighter," Irene said through the phone.

"If you saw him, you would understand why she's doing it," Cynthia chimed in. "I mean you might as well call that man sexual chocolate. I may be married, but that don't mean I've gone blind."

"Is he that fine?" Irene asked.

"You know the stuff those firemen calendars are made of? The ones we don't think are actual firemen because none of the ones we've seen in real life ever look like the ones in the calendar? Yeah, that's him. He can be in all twelve damn months, and I'd still buy every copy I could."

I howled with laughter. "Imma tell Marcel on you."

Cynthia took a sip of her wine and shrugged. "Tell him. The man likes a good challenge."

Irene screamed through the phone, and we all erupted with laughter.

"He must be something if he got you cooking and shit," Irene commented.

I finished chopping up the herbs and tossed them into my roux. "I told both you heifers that I was simply being friendly. Nothing more nothing less."

"Uh-huh. Right. T-bone steaks, pan-roasted carrots, baked potato, and I believe it was a red velvet cake I saw you finishing up when I got here. Yeah, just being friendly my ass." Cynthia took another drink, but not before I saw the knowing smirk on her lips.

Irene brought the mood down with her next comment. "I still can't believe it, Regina. And it makes no damn sense. I'm sorry I couldn't get away. But I should be there this weekend."

I let out a heavy sigh. "I appreciate it, Irene. But you don't really need to fly down here. I know you busy and all with patients to see cuz you're a big-time doctor."

"Gurl please, it's family medicine, nothing super exciting. And to be honest, I could use some time away from a lot of things."

Cynthia and I glanced at each other, again picking up the hint of melancholy in her voice. It'd seemed to be there a lot in the last couple months, not to mention she wasn't always so quick to mute her phone before she and Derrick got into some random tiff or another. Anytime we'd attempted to ask she always had one excuse or another behind the it's all fine comments.

"Well, if you do come, I only have two guests booked in at the B&B this weekend, so you can take the other room. If you don't want to stay with your folks that is," Cynthia said. She glanced at her phone, then drained the rest of her wine. "I better get out of here before your booty call shows up."

I tossed a dishrag in her direction, and she ducked, laughing.

"What! You can't go. I need to be on the phone when he arrives. I need to see this man for myself," Irene protested.

"Both of y'all are acting like me getting a little D is something new. Y'all know better."

"True, true. But this is the first one you've cooked for. And the first one you've had come to your house," Cynthia pointed out.

"Don't matter. I didn't invite him over for that. I am being friendly. With no benefits," I added before either of them said anything.

But she wasn't wrong. While I wasn't living the life of a devoted widow, I also kept my dalliances separate. Technology had made the no-strings-attached life much easier. Dinner, dancing, light dates here or there, but nothing more serious than that, and the sex always happened at their place. I got what I needed and took my ass home to sleep in my own bed. Alone. Anytime they even hinted at something more than casual I cut them off. I'd had my child and the bakery, and no time for a man who'd be wanting attention I didn't have to give. Not that it mattered. Inviting Alec over wasn't a big deal. My dinner with him wasn't about sex, it was strictly a cordial invite regardless of what my friends or libido hinted at.

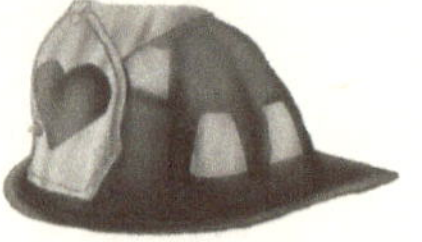

ALEC

I stood outside the brick Tudor-style home and adjusted the packages in my hand. Wine and flowers. I'd been unsure if I should bring anything since this wasn't a date, but I didn't want to show up empty-handed. I'd jumped at her invitation for a few reasons. The volunteer guys operated differently. There had been no cooking rotation. Some of the guys had meals prepared and labeled in the fridge, but mostly it was stocked with quick easy to make microwave things. After a few days I'd already grown tired of eating frozen meals and junk food so a home cooked meal would be nice. And the company would be even nicer. I ran my hand down my face, rolled my shoulders back, and then pushed the button.

A click of a lock and then the door swung open. "Well damn. When you said with bells on looks like you meant it."

"It'd be rude to be late. And my mom raised me better than that."

She smiled and stepped to the side to let me in. Gone were the bright-orange scrubs with mini cupcakes and cakes all over them. They'd been replaced with a long red button-down shirt that stopped mid-thigh, paired with gray leggings. Like on the previous occasions when I'd seen Miss Parker, her lipstick matched her outfit, and the deep-ruby color looked like a flashing beacon, drawing me in and tempting me for a kiss.

"For you." I handed her the bouquet of colorful daisies and the Pinot Noir I'd picked up from the store.

"Oh, look at you trying to woo me."

"Yes, ma'am. You were kind enough to offer me dinner, I wouldn't dare show up here empty-handed."

"Ma'am? Stop trying to make me feel older than I am. I told you you're young, but not that young." She held a mischievous glint in her eye when she said those words.

I licked my lips and smiled. "I doubt you've felt old a day in your life. Sure as hell don't look it. And speaking of my age, just how old do you think I am?"

Her eyes roamed the length of my body, and a smirk graced those kissable lips. My clothing selection was limited, but I was glad I packed some casual wear for my time here. My navy-blue polo shirt, light wash jeans, and white Converse said relaxed, but that I'd still put some effort in.

"I give you thirty."

I stroked my goatee and grinned. She was close. "Not bad. Thirty-two actually, but not bad."

She hmphed, then turned and headed deeper into the house. Her place was about what I would expect. Neat and homey with some pops of color that seemed to reflect her personality. A large sixty-inch flat screen hung above the fireplace, and there were photos on the mantel, but as we passed, I couldn't get a good glimpse of who was featured.

"Damn, smells good in here," I said as we got closer to the kitchen.

"Thank ya. Thank ya. And it'll taste even better."

She set the wine and flowers on her oversized island and started looking under the cabinets, opening and closing doors until she came up with a vase. She then opened a drawer and turned to hand me a bottle opener.

"You gotta put in some of the work." She placed two glasses next to the bottle.

I eased around the island, moving closer to my voluptuous host. She hummed to herself as she filled the vase and arranged the flowers. I found myself somewhat amazed at her resilience. She'd lost her business temporarily, yet she was holding it together. Granted, I'd not seen her initial reaction to the loss, but so many times I've witnessed the crying, screaming, and heartbreak firsthand on the job. Was Regina Parker the kind of woman who broke down?

She turned and a frown pulled at the corners of her mouth. "Why are you staring at me?"

"I was just thinking."

She inched closer; her fingers brushed against mine when she took the glass I offered. "About?"

"You."

"Hm-hm, what about me?" She tipped the glass to her lips, and I zeroed in on them.

There was an attraction between us. A low buzz of arousal zinging under the surface, ready to be set free. Or at least I hoped that's what was happening here.

"About what you've been through. I'm sorry someone set your place on fire."

She sighed and turned away; the flirtatious energy evaporated when she started plating the food. "Shit happens, I guess."

I stepped closer but didn't crowd her space. "I realize I'm not from around here, but the chief sings your praises. And with the line of people I saw this morning, I have a hard time imagining anyone who'd want to hurt you in such a way."

Regina picked up the two dishes and carried them over to the table. I grabbed the wineglasses and bottle to follow.

"That's kind of you to say."

I meant every word. It'd only been a handful of days, but the woman sitting across from me had a pull, like everyone wanted to be in her orbit. Maybe it was the pastries, but the few interactions I'd had with her from the butting of heads to the subtle flirting...it didn't matter. I'd enjoyed each moment and had been sucked in from the first day.

However, there was something. The shift in her mood, the downplaying of what happened. There was more under the surface, and I found myself wanting to know what. But she didn't know me like that, so I didn't expect any sort of heart-to-heart soulful confessions.

"Are you planning to do another bake sale?"

"Are you going to chastise me if I do?"

She cut a piece of her steak and slowly closed her lips around it, keeping her gaze locked on me. My pants grew tighter in response. I picked up my wine and took a sip while shifting ever so slightly hoping to readjust and alleviate some of the discomfort.

"Would you want me to?"

Regina gave me an appraising glance while continuing to eat her food. "Not sure I know you well enough, yet, Mr. Special Investigator, to have that particular conversation."

"Are there some sort of checkpoints I need to hit before we get to that level?"

"Maybe. Though I may have some concerns about you being up to the task."

All I could do was laugh at her comment. There was something about Regina Parker, something that made conversation easy. Maybe it was her call-it-like-she-sees-it attitude or that there were no pretenses between us. Regardless, spending time with her was the highlight of my time in this little town. We ate, joked, and generally had a pleasant meal.

"Guess you didn't like it," she commented with a playful smile as she looked at my empty plate.

I shook my head and returned the grin. "Worst meal I've had in ages."

She pushed back from the table and gathered our empty plates. I stood and took them from her hands. "Here, let me."

"Just put them next to the sink. I'll clean up later."

"You sure you don't want me to help you now?"

She leaned against the countertop and folded her arms across her chest. "Are you trying to stall so you can stay at my house longer?"

I moved toward her, leaving a little space, but close enough that if she gave the slightest indication, I could finally taste the lips I've been mesmerized with all night. "Well, I haven't had dessert yet. I mean, I did come for a little bit of sugar."

Regina closed the space between us, tilting her chin up while licking her lips. "And sugar you shall have."

Then she was gone. Around the island and over to the cake stand that housed a beautifully decorated red velvet. One of my favorites. It was stunning, she had skill. It looked like one of the ones I'd see on the cooking shows mom watched. It had the fancy icing roses around the perimeter with chopped pecan pieces covering the top. Around the bottom of the cake was the typical red crumb coating, the tell-tale sign signaling the good-ness inside. She cut a generous slice and placed it on one of the saucers, then pushed it across the surface toward me. Not exactly the dessert I had in mind, but as she moved over to the living room, I figured it'd be the only kind I'd get.

Regina opened the cabinet of the built in, and I wasn't ashamed to admit I was slightly bummed when she kneeled to look at the contents instead of bending over. She had a nice ass, and I more than enjoyed looking at it every chance I could.

Leaving the cake behind, I refilled our glasses, emptying the bottle, and carried them over to her just as music started pouring out of well-hidden speakers. Not just any music, but Otis Redding on vinyl. She started swaying to his soulful voice and silently thanked me as she took her glass.

"Do you mind?" I asked, pointing to the cabinet.

She shook her head and opened the door she'd just been searching. Her record collection was impressive.

"What's old is new again," Regina stated. "But some of those

I've had for years, well before you youngins decided records were the new hip thing."

I took her glass and set both on one of the shelves, then slid my hand around her waist. I'd wanted to have this woman in my arms since the morning I'd met her, and this moment provided me the perfect opportunity.

I held her close and began moving us to the slow, romantic tune. Her body was divine, soft and feminine. We fell into an easy rhythm that didn't need words, and the more we moved, the more she relaxed into me. When I started singing along to "Cigarettes and Coffee," she leaned back.

"What you know about Otis?"

"There are quite a few things I know about, Ms. Parker, but... I'm not sure I know you well enough for that particular conversation."

7

REGINA

I WOULD NOT ALLOW MYSELF TO ACKNOWLEDGE THE SULLEN mood that acted like a gray cloud above me all day. Instead, I would focus on how well my staff pulled together so we could have yet another "bake sale" as Special Investigator Hodge called it. I couldn't stop the smile that formed on my lips thinking about him, though. The date—no, scratch that. Not a date. Dinner; it was simply dinner—had been nice. The type of evening that I had not had in a long time.

Especially the dancing. I don't know what possessed me to put music on, but if he was stalling on leaving, I'd figured why not. And the man could move. That much had been evident as he easily transitioned from a slow jam to something more upbeat and back again as the record played.

"He got you looking all dreamy," Cynthia said.

"Who?" Momma questioned. I swear that woman had ears like a hawk. We weren't even that close to her, yet she perked up soon as she got a hint of possible gossip.

"Nobody. I'm just tired so I'm looking spacey, not dreamy."

"Uh-huh right." Cynthia rolled her eyes and finished breaking down the last folding table. Again, making me thankful for her help. I knew she didn't have to be here, out in the sun with me

36

trying to do whatever I could to keep this fire from taking the business under, but she was. My employee Nick strolled over to grab the table, saving us from having to lug it to the trailer.

"Now, what's going on?"

"Nothing, Momma."

She crossed her arms and pushed her lips out and pinned me with the stare that shouldn't have still been an effective tool on me at my age. But sadly, it was.

"Ain't nothing. Cynthia over here trying to make a mountain out of a molehill because I had dinner with Alec last night."

"Alec? I don't know no Alec."

I sighed and rolled the tension from my neck. "The guy, Momma. The one poking around in the building the last few days."

"Oh...oh. Yeah, he's cute. Your niece was talking about him as she drove us home. And you done already snagged him. Didn't waste no time."

I shot Cynthia a glare as she leaned against the back of her truck laughing. She started this whole mess.

"She snagged who?" Tricia asked.

"The cute young...well, young for me, too old for you, fireman."

"Oohh go head, Auntie."

I shook my head and ignored all of them. Besides, it had just been dinner. No expectations, which meant no disappointments. Just dinner. And a one-time thing. His investigation was done, which meant he was probably either already back in Savannah or close to being there. *Just dinner*.

However, thinking about him reminded me I needed to thank the guys at the firehouse. They'd done the best they could to save what could be saved. The building probably would have been a total loss, and I would be rebuilding from the ground up if not for them. Plus, they'd kept the damage contained to just me, and it hadn't spread to my neighbor. They had some water damage, but that was the extent. I had to remind myself it could have been worse even though my heart ached every time I looked at my shop. But I knew this was only a temporary setback.

This would not beat me.

After I got home, I decided to whip up a batch of brownies and cookies. It wasn't a lot, but it'd be better than nothing, and once we were up and running again, they could have all the free coffee and pastries they wanted.

On the drive to the firehouse, I made a mental checklist of all the things I needed to get done. I needed to talk to the chief about when I could have the report so I could get it to my insurance company so we could get that process started. Paperwork and red tape were always a fucking headache, but it had to be done. In my rough, and probably hopeful estimation, we'd be closed for at least six months. The thought of spending half a year pretty much out of business sat like an anchor in my stomach. The pop-up back-lot selling couldn't sustain us for that long.

Tricia had mentioned doing one of those online fundraiser sites, but I wasn't fully comfortable with the idea. Our setback was temporary. We were getting some outside support thanks to the followers from the bakery Instagram. She'd posted pictures, and folks had chimed in asking how to help. Plus, the community was leaving us donations outside of making purchases. I would leave the fundraiser sites to people who were more in need.

I pulled into the side parking lot of the red brick building and killed the engine. I got the plastic containers from the back and headed inside. A couple of the guys were sitting around a card table playing Spades. When they saw me, they waved, and Harold jogged over to relieve me of my packages.

Their faces lit up as soon as they opened the lids, and they began talking about how glad they were to be on duty tonight. I started to ask if Chief Morris was around when he came walking past the large fire truck with none-other than Special Investigator Hodge in tow.

"Regina," Chief said, arms wide open to embrace me. "I would ask what you're doing here, but I can see from the guys already stuffing their faces."

"Yeah, nothing major. Just wanted to offer up a thank-you for everything."

"We were just doin' our jobs. Sorry we couldn't save more of it, though."

"You did what you could, and I appreciate it. It'll be fine, though. I'll be back before you know it."

"I have no doubt, no doubt at all." He turned to face Alec. "You think about what I said, okay?"

Alec smiled and nodded before the chief said his goodbyes and headed out the bay door.

"I expected you to be gone."

Alec grinned wide and stuck his arm out, inclining his head toward large glass double doors that led to the interior of the station. "Do you think I'd leave without saying goodbye?"

I shrugged and walked in the direction he'd indicated. "I don't see why not. It's not like you owe me anything."

"True. How about this, I didn't want to leave without saying goodbye. I was going to call you once I got done here, but you've arrived instead. It must be fate."

I wouldn't let myself acknowledge the almost happy feeling at seeing him. Stress. It had to be stress. That was the only thing that made sense because I didn't know him from Adam, so this uncharacteristic excitement made no sense. Not to mention, I shouldn't have cared that he planned to call me, or so he'd said.

I followed him deeper into the building until we got to the small room that was about the size of Darnell's dormitory before he'd moved into an apartment with his girlfriend. There was an uncomfortable looking twin-size bed, small desk, lamp, and dresser. Bare bones, but a place to lay your head. On the bed sat a duffel bag and the computer satchel he'd been carrying around. I dropped my purse beside it.

He closed the door behind us. "Did you get all dressed up to see me?"

I looked down at my outfit. The denim blue sleeveless dress was more for comfort than anything. The material was soft and didn't cling to my body and had pockets. I loved a dress with pockets. If he thought this was dressed up, I'd blow his poor mind when I really put effort in.

"Considering I expected you to be gone already, not really, but if it makes you feel better to think otherwise, by all means, yes, I dressed up just to impress you, Special Investigator."

He closed the distance between us. Like last night, the undercurrent of lust and curiosity buzzed between us.

He placed a hand on my hip, and the corner of his mouth lifted into a devastatingly sexy half-smile. "It does. It makes me feel so much better."

The hint of sweet wafting off him mixed with a tinge of ginger and a little tobacco like from an expensive cigar teased my senses. Last night we'd teetered on the edge, but we'd both practiced a restraint that kept us from falling over. But I wanted to let go. And the way his attention was zeroed in on my lips, I had the feeling he wanted the same thing.

"Are you going to kiss me now, or..."

I didn't get the chance to finish the sentence as his lips descended on mine. They were soft, yet firm. Alec slipped his tongue into my mouth on a slow exploration while he inched his hands down to grab my ass. I slid my arms under his, clawing at his back.

The hairs of his goatee tickled my face. My heart raced, and I was near dizzy, drunk on the hedonistic kiss. He retreated and I advanced. Our tongues moved in a synchronized tango. Bodies close, I was aware of him and how his dick hardened between us. I moaned and pressed tighter.

Alec pulled away, our breathing ragged and his pupils dilated. His Adam's apple bobbled when he swallowed. "We keep this up,

Ms. Parker, and I'm liable to have you sweating off your makeup."

"Is that a promise? Because you shouldn't go making claims you can't back up."

His dazzling white teeth went on full display, and he shot a side glance toward the door. "Are you a screamer?"

"Only one way to find out."

 8

ALEC

I brushed my lips against her ear. "I'd hate to sully your reputation in this quaint little town of yours."

Regina ran a hand down my chest until she stroked my dick through my quickly tightening pants. "If you're scared, just say so. But I'm a whole grown ass woman that can happily get hers and walk out with her head held high."

She stared me dead in the eyes as she spoke the words. This was not the sendoff I'd imagined, but hell if I'd turn it down.

"Tell Daddy how you like it."

She jerked back. "Daddy? Now I know you been dealing with just them young ones. You ain't ready."

Regina stepped back and looked me up and down. I suppressed a smile, knowing that the comment did as intended and got a rise out of the feisty Ms. Parker. My dick ached painfully, screaming out for relief. I advanced, grabbing her at the waist and spinning us so I pushed her against the wall. I ground my erection into her while running my hand up until I made contact with the glorious breasts I'd been admiring from day one. Her nipple grew hard beneath the fabric, and I pinched the stiff bud. Damn if I didn't want her naked and spread out so I could have full access to her wonderland of a body.

"You think I can't handle you?" I whispered harshly into her ear.

She responded by pushing her ass back and gyrating, drawing a long groan from me.

"I've had plenty that were all talk and little to no game." Regina glanced back over her shoulder. "Prove me wrong."

Fuck. I didn't think I could get any harder, but three words did just that. It may have been presumptuous of me, but I was damn glad I'd picked up condoms in hopes dinner had led somewhere. As much as I hated to remove my hands from her, I undid my pants, and the relief was instant. I pulled my wallet from my pocket, grabbed the latex, then rolled it on with her watching my every move.

I dove in for another kiss and ran my hand between her legs. When I reached the damp fabric of her panties, I smiled against her lips. "So wet." I pressed my thumb against her, making small circles. I kissed along her jawline and down her neck. "And say what you want, but you dressed in this for me." I slid my hand inside her panties and cupped her pussy. "You wanted me last night. And you sure as hell want me now."

I dipped a finger inside and continued the leisurely stroking of her clit. God, she was so wet and ready, her arousal making it easy to move in and out of her slick body.

I stared at her as I slowly added another digit, fucking her with my fingers. She parted her lips and soft mewling sounds bubbled out of her.

A grin tugged at the corner of my mouth. "You can do better than that, Ms. Parker. I want this whole fucking town to hear you screaming my name."

She tilted her chin up and smirked. "Put your money where your mouth is."

I stepped back and spun her so she once again faced the wall. Yanking her hips toward me, I shoved her panties to the side and slammed into her. She yelped in surprise but pushed her ass back into my thrusts. Her warm body hugged my dick in a pleasure grip. I dug my fingers into her sides, pounding into her hard and fast.

"Fuck! Yes." She groaned, beating her fist against the cinderblock wall. "That's it. Show Momma whatcha made of."

No surprise she'd turned it around on me, but her demand was like a lightning bolt electrifying my animalistic desires to new heights. My breaths were forced out in hot pants. I squeezed her ass, then ran my thumb between the cheeks until I got to the tight little hole and pressed against it. I didn't breach, but it was enough; she arched her back and drew in a sharp gasp. She responded to ass play. Ms. Parker was full of surprises.

I bent my knees and tilted my hips up on the next thrust and got what I was after.

"Alec...oh, sweet...yes, right there...right fucking there."

My balls tightened. I was close. Faster I went. She shoved a hand between her legs to play with herself while slightly rotating her hips. The music of flesh against flesh was accompanied by grunts and moans. The heady aroma of sex swirled in the air.

"Alec, fuck...keep going." Regina braced her arm rod straight as her body trembled around me. The hand in her panties continued moving as she rode out the waves of her release.

I kept going. My fingers dug into her waist as I pumped harder. The tiny tremors from her pussy massaged my dick, teasing me closer and closer. She gripped my wrist as she arched her back. A low "shit" rumbled from her throat. My heart pounded, I thrust hard and stilled, groaning low and deep as I filled the condom.

Neither of us moved. Sweat dripped down my face, and a thin sheen coated her arms. Once the room stopped spinning, I eased out, pulling free with a soft, wet pop. Regina stumbled the short distance to the bed and collapsed. I gathered my pants and wide legged walked over to the trash to discard the used latex.

"You alright?"

She huffed an airy laugh while staring up at the ceiling.

"Yeah. I'm more than alright. Damn, I needed that." She pushed herself into a seated position and reached for her bag.

Was she leaving already? Before I could formulate why that idea might have bothered me, she pulled out a smaller pouch and gave herself a quick wipe-down with some sort of towelette. A woman prepared.

"You need me to get you anything?"

She smiled. Her face had a post orgasmic glow, relaxed, sated. I couldn't help the pride that bloomed in my ego at being the cause of it.

Regina stood and straightened her clothes. "You already got me what I needed. Been hella stressed, as you can imagine." She sauntered over to me and stretched up to kiss me lightly then tossed the used towelette and wrapper into the trash. "I'm good. And you need to get on the road."

Ouch. Damn. I don't think I'd ever been so dismissed. While we both knew this was just a quick hookup, I guess I'd expected something more. Something seemingly less transactional.

I wrapped my arms around her waist. "I'm in no hurry. We can go back to your place and..."

She pulled free and walked over to gather up her purse. "You pack a punch, Special Investigator, I'll give you that. And I wouldn't mind another round...at another time."

It could have been my bruised ego's imagination, but while she'd said the words in the same flirtatious manner as before, they seemed more forced.

"Drive safely, and if you're ever in town again, give me a call."

With a parting kiss, she was out the door.

✤ 9 ✤

REGINA

THE THUNDER RATTLED THE WINDOWS OF THE SMALL SHERIFF'S station. It'd been raining non-stop for days, which made doing the parking lot bakery impossible. Irene's visit had kept me somewhat occupied, but after she'd left, sitting around with idle hands gave me way too much time to wallow in my situation. When Momma walked in, I stood and smoothed down my over-sized shirt. I'd told her I could handle the visit on my own, but even though she was retired and I was in charge, the bakery was still her baby. Though I shouldn't be surprised because my grand-mother had been the same way, and if I would admit it to myself, I probably would be as well after I handed the reins over to Tricia.

"Sorry I'm late. With all this rain your daddy don't know what to do with himself so he needs to talk to me about every little thing all the damn time no matter what I tell him I got to do."

She made a big show of rolling her eyes and sighing dramati-cally, but after forty plus years of marriage, my parents were still very much in love. They had the happy relationship I'd thought I would have had, but the universe cruelly had other plans. I shook off those thoughts. Life was what life was and dwelling on the past did me no favors. I picked up my purse off the bench, which had all the files from the accountant, plus the report from Alec, ready to lay it out for the sheriff to see where we went next.

"No worries, Momma. Pops is on a call."

Just as I said the words, the man I still considered my father-in-law opened his door, stepped out of his office, and beckoned to us.

"Regina, Mabel, so sorry to keep you waiting."

We strolled past a few desks, waving at the deputies. Miss Lucille, the sheriff's admin, and really the backbone of the entire station, smiled at us as we passed. In the last month and a half, I had been inside these walls more than I had in my entire forty-three years living on Madison Island. Like Chief Morris, Sheriff Fredrick Parker probably should have retired a good five years ago, but in a place that saw little to no action on any front, sitting behind that desk gave him purpose. I suspected I was the center of the most scandal this town had seen in twenty years if not longer. First, the grand larceny, and now with the arson.

For the most part, he was a stoic man, but the image of him breaking down on my doorstep when he delivered the news that I'd lost my husband and he'd lost his wife was burned into my memory. In one fell swoop our family had been forever devastatingly changed. Like me, he'd handled his grief by throwing himself into his work and also spending more time with Darnell. It wasn't that he'd not been a doting grandfather before, but his interactions with my son changed and I understood. Knowing we could have lost him as well, we'd clung to that little boy.

"How are you two holding up?"

Mom shifted in her seat and squared her shoulders. "Best as could be expected considering our livelihood is in rubble."

He shook his head. "That's a damn shame. And Pat said the young fella he had come down suspects arson."

I dug into my bag to pull out the report Alec had emailed me and fought hard to keep the smile off my face thinking about the last time I'd seen him. I handed the paper to the sheriff. "I think it was Trent." I spoke my suspicions out loud for the first time, and Momma grabbed my hand.

"You think he's capable of something like this?" she asked with eyes wide.

"It's the only thing that makes sense. He's been fired, charged, and all but run out of town once everything made the paper. Who else?"

Pops rested his forearms on his desk and clucked his tongue three times. His nostrils flared at the mention of my ex-employee's name. He'd had his deputy do the arrest and interrogation because he hadn't trusted himself not to kick Trent's ass over what he'd done.

"Yeah, it does make sense he'd be suspect number one. Let me scratch up his address from the bond hearing. Think he was staying with family down in Augusta. Good thing, too, if it was him that did it." The wrinkles on his forehead deepened when his bushy gray eyebrows pinched together, and his lips turned into a snarl. "Marcus is still in charge of the case, but I'll reach out and get back with you."

I had no doubt Pops would do his job—he had with the first incident—but this one was worse. This one left me unable to keep busy and pushing forward. This one reminded me every day what a fool I'd been.

He stood and rounded his desk. "We're going to get him. That I can promise."

I rose and hugged him, and Momma did the same.

"You better throw not just the book, but the whole damn library at him, Freddie," she said. "And please call and talk to Al so he'll give me some peace," she added with another dramatic eye roll. "I swear I don't know why he couldn't keep working like the rest of you old geezers."

I shook my head, and Pops threw his hands up. Once I ushered her from the office and promised to have dinner with Pops, Momma and I parted ways after she lectured me again about beating myself up over everything. That woman had an uncanny ability to know what I was thinking. By the time I made it home, the rain had finally let up. Some time in my garden would do me good. Next to baking, tending to my plants was my place of peace.

The expansive backyard was a point of pride for me after years of careful planning and grooming. Fragrant flowers, shade trees, fruits, vegetables, and herbs all had a carefully laid out home. And my favorite spot was the pergola at the far end, which housed my swinging bench. Many a night had been spent out there, sipping on a beverage and simply enjoying the peace.

The Tudor style hadn't appealed to either of us, but once I'd laid eyes on the yard and the potential it held, Lawrence had known it was the house we'd be buying. A rueful smile tugged at my lips. Making me happy had always been his top priority. And while the pain had dulled over the years, when times were stressful like now, I missed him as if the accident were yesterday. Lawrence had always been my calm. My safe place. My comfort. And somehow, no matter how annoyed I might have been, he'd find a way to make me smile. To remind me that whatever crisis we were dealing with would pass.

I needed him. Tears burned my eyes, but I swallowed them down. No more wallowing. This too would pass. Earbuds in place, I cranked up my music and focused my attention on plucking some ripe blueberries and mint to make a couple jars of jam. Figured it'd pair well with the biscuits I was planning to make for Cynthia's guests. My heart warmed with pride over how well my friend's B&B had taken off. People wanting weekend getaways, not to mention she was up and coming as a wedding location. Our small town was getting noticed, which made the timing of the fire ten times worse.

Not only was I losing out on the regular business that had kept us thriving since the bakery first opened, but also the new —although minimum—tourist traffic. The fancy new website Cynthia had advised I get had also helped. I had three wedding cakes on the books for the next two months because of it. Which I'd forgotten about until this very fucking moment.

"Shit." I sat back on my heels and glanced up to the gray sky. A large raindrop hit my face.

I pushed to standing, gathered up my stuff, and made it to the covered patio before the downpour started. When it rains it pours had never been so fucking spot on. After toeing off my gardening clogs, I carried my wicker basket of goodies into the house when my phone started buzzing in my pocket. Seeing my son's number was the ray of sunshine I needed.

I leaned against the counter and answered. "Hey baby, how's it goin'?"

"Good, good. Just wanted to call and see how you're doing."

"Hanging in there. Had to go to the station and talk to Pops today, then just got through with a little gardening before the skies opened up again."

"Hold up. The way you said that doesn't sound like a simple family visit." The alarm in his voice deepened it.

I sighed. I didn't want him to worry, but I also wouldn't lie to him about this. Downplay maybe, but never lie. "Alec found evidence of arson. I needed to follow up with Pops about that."

"Alec? Oh, that dude you were flirting with."

I straightened to full height, not that he could see me or that it would have mattered since his six-four self had dwarfed me since he turned twelve. Folks always talked about how it was a shame he had no coordination for sports. He had my genes to thank for that.

"There was no flirting." There had been a lot of flirting plus a little stress relief, though my nineteen-year-old did not need to know any of that.

"Whatever, Ma. It might be good for you. But back to the arson. Seriously? Do they know who? Do I need to come home? Are you okay?"

I walked over and took a seat at the table. His concern made my entire being weary. The older he got, the more he reminded me of his father, and not just in looks. His mannerisms and the sound of his voice, especially in times of stress. I massaged at the dull throb starting in my temples. I ran through my suspicions, with him being briefly offended I'd not told him about Trent. But in my defense, it went down at the end of his semester, and the only thing I'd wanted him worried about was passing his finals and completing his first year of college.

After we hung up, I rested my head on my folded arms on top of the table. Just as the tiredness started to settle on me, I popped up as something Darnell had said replayed in my mind. What the hell had he meant it might be good for me?

❦ 10 ❦

ALEC

"Hodge. Get your butt in here," Chief Johnson yelled soon as my boots crossed the threshold into the house.

I waved my acknowledgment and headed toward his office, murmuring hellos to my fellow firefighters.

Being back on the schedule was exactly what I needed. Chilling around my place had left me with too much time to replay my last interaction with Regina Parker. She'd walked out. No cuddling, no asking when we'd see each other again, nothing. She'd gotten off and left. That fact messed with my head more than it should have. And I didn't understand why.

No strings was what I lived for. Many a night I'd gone out with my buddy Reggie and hooked up with a woman, or two. Mutual sex, but only sex. That's how I rolled. Much to my mother's displeasure, I was content with the bachelor life. Yet, Regina giving me exactly that had surprisingly left me a bit stunned.

I forced the thoughts away as I put my bag on the floor and settled into the peeling, rickety chair across from Chief's desk.

"So, how'd it go?" he asked, folding his hands together and peering at me with his ice-blue eyes.

Being back here brought the stark comparisons between the two top men. Chief Morris was laid back and really only acted as a figurehead, as opposed to Chief Johnson, who was still very much in the mix. Sort of. He showed up at calls to supervise on occasion, especially if it was a larger blaze, but for the most part he was more admin.

I leaned back in the chair, the metal creaking beneath my weight. "It went well. Definitely arson. Left a copy of the report with Chief Morris."

"Think it's the owner trying to defraud the insurance?"

I knew it was a reasonable question. Hell, it was a thought I'd had myself before meeting said owner. But an unreasonable flash of annoyance struck me.

I shifted, widening my legs, and brushing invisible lint from my dark blue cargo pants. "Nah. She seemed on the up and up. Apparently, it's a family business four generations strong. Regina didn't do it."

Chief Johnson sat up straighter. "Regina? Got cozy while there, did you?"

I kept my features schooled. Getting cozy wasn't exactly what I'd call it. "Let's just say the people in that town are real...casual."

He folded his arms and stared me down for a moment. "Welp," he finally said, drumming his hands on his desk. "This is all wrapped up then?"

"Should be. I mean if they have any questions, I left my information with Chief Morris so he can get in touch."

"Make sure you keep your files. I's dotted and t's crossed should you need to testify once they catch the arsonist."

I understood the dismissal, grabbed my bag, and headed out of the office. My next two days would be spent in the bunkroom. Upside, I was on shift with Tyler, who was by far the best cook of the bunch of us, including Sasha. At least being at work would keep me occupied so I could easily ignore Regina's number taunting me to call. Other than a polite thank you when I'd emailed her my findings, and despite the fact she had all my contact information, she'd not reached out, and I now found myself in a one-sided game of chicken.

❧

WHAT THE HELL was I doing? I'd been asking myself that same question since I got up this morning and had the bug in my ass to head back to the tiny, hole-in-the-wall town. Even as I approached the downtown square area, I had no answer other than two weeks later, Regina Parker had remained on my mind, and I wouldn't be satisfied until I saw her again.

After a little bit of searching, I managed to find a parking spot. As I walked down the sidewalk, the yellow caution tape around her store blew in the slight breeze. A sobering thought hit me at the sight; someone had done that to her place.

I rounded the corner to see a few people hanging around while others broke down what was left of her parking lot pop-up shop. A few upgrades had been made in the form of one of those portable tents seen at tailgating events. At least she had some shade to work in now. I scanned the small crowd until my eyes settled on the woman in question. She stood next to a white Ford pickup talking to a tall bald man. She wore more super colorful scrubs. Her dreads were expertly piled atop her head and secured with an equally colorful but perfectly coordinated scarf. They laughed and conversed easily. Too easily.

"Ooh, what's got your nostrils a flaring?"

I glanced to the side to see Regina's mother smiling at me. The older woman grinned like a Cheshire cat as she looked in the direction my attention had just been. Deep lines crinkled around her eyes; a playful expression remained on her face.

"Oh, baby, don't be jealous," she said, linking her arm in mine. "That's just Marcel, they more like siblings. Besides, that most eligible bachelor has been snatched off the market. We weren't properly introduced last time. I'm Mabel. Mabel Charles."

I let her lead me toward a table where Regina's friend stood talking to a younger girl, who also looked to be related to the woman on my arm and the one I'd come to see.

"Tricia, we got any of them cookies left? Mr. Firefighter man here could use a little sweetness to cut his bitter mood."

Heat rolled through my body that had nothing to do with the quickly rising Georgia September temperature. Tricia smiled at me then quickly turned to check the boxes stacked on a chair.

"Good to see you again. What brings you back to town," Cynthia asked.

"I..."

"Look like he came to fight your Marcel for Gina's honor. Face all scrunched, nose flaring."

The older woman squawked out a laugh and tapped my arm. The other two smiled, and the younger handed me a cellophane bag tied with a green ribbon, which held three cookies. Being the butt of their joke stung a little, but it wasn't totally misplaced. I had been unreasonably annoyed over the interaction I'd witnessed.

Cynthia and Tricia moved to start breaking down the tent. "I can help." I set the cookies on the table, and the three of us got it down with Regina's mom giving instruction.

We'd just finished when the pair in question came over.

"Here, I'll take it." The man who'd been identified as Marcel said, holding his arms out for the large, awkward covering.

A younger guy helped him carry it over to a trailer that now sat in the corner of the lot. The few stragglers were taking the tables and chairs over as well. She really did have a whole operation going on, which was impressive.

"Didn't expect to see you here, Special Investigator," Regina said in greeting.

The other women snickered among themselves, but luckily none of them repeated anything Ms. Charles had said minutes earlier.

"Just doing some follow up." Wasn't a total lie.

"Oh, so the insurance lady contacted you then?"

I tilted my head and frowned. "No."

She put her hands on her hips. Hips I instantly recalled digging my fingers into... Before I could go too far down memory lane, Marcel returned and Tricia got my attention, holding out the cookies again so they could break down the last table. The man, who had a very distinct black band around his left ring finger, officially introduced himself to me. Cynthia whispered something in his ear when he went to kiss her cheek, which got me another look and a small laugh. So, I wasn't going to be embarrassed in front of Regina, but that didn't mean my apparent facial expressions were going to go unmentioned.

"What is going on with y'all?" Regina asked.

"I think..."

"Nothin'," Tricia broke in, cutting off Regina's mom and getting a stern look in return that nearly made the younger woman recoil. "Come on, GG, you been out in the sun too long. It's time to get you home before I head back to school."

I appreciated she was attempting to save me from further embarrassment, but I did worry she was likely to get a lecture during that car ride. However, she seemed less bothered as she gave me a small smile and wave while ushering the fussing older woman away.

"Now I know something is up," Regina said, shifting her eyes from me to her friend.

"You know how much of a busy body your momma is," Cynthia stated.

Regina pushed her lime-green tinted lips into a pout while narrowing her eyes at both of us. "Uh-huh. Y'all ain't slick. But I'm too hot to be worried about y'all's foolishness right now."

Marcel returned and slid his hand along Cynthia's lower back. "You ready?"

She nodded, gave her friend a departing hug, said her good-byes to me, then they left. The couple hadn't even pulled off before Regina turned her focus back to me.

"Why are you here if you haven't heard from my insurance company?"

"I just wanted to check on you. See how you were."

A playful grin tugged the corner of her mouth upward. "You came all this way when a phone call would do?"

She arched one of her perfectly shaped brows. The action once again made me question what had possessed me to make the trip. But it was too late to second guess now.

"Are you saying you're not happy to see me?"

She shook her head. "Not saying that at all."

It was a little admission, but it was a start. And it made me feel like less of a needy fool for showing up.

REGINA

I APPLIED A FINAL COAT OF MY NEW MAUVE LIPSTICK, PRESSED my lips together to ensure even coverage, then swiped my thumb along the bottom to clean up any smudges. Being late was not my MO, but I'd be borderline thanks to my indecisiveness on outfits. It was lunch. Just lunch, and here I was overthinking what the hell I was going to wear.

I turned to the side to check my reflection. The dark washed jeans were my favorite. They made my ass look spectacular, and the high waist showed off my shape, helping to draw attention to my curvy hips. Not to mention they were comfortable. That was key because I hated the ones that dug in when I sat down.

I adjusted my tits, making sure my cleavage was on point. Special Investigator liked staring at the girls, so the shirt I'd picked would be the perfect tease. The light pink sheer material would catch his eye, but the matching tank would keep too much from sight. I was a respectable lady, after all.

I laughed at that thought, considering the guys from the firehouse had a hard time looking me in the eye for a few days. More their problem than mine, though. I glanced back at the alarm clock. "Shit!" I grabbed my phone, purse, and keys, then darted out of my room.

Luckily, the drive to Vito's was only ten minutes, so I wouldn't be too late. Alec had come to see me. I wasn't the type to get caught up in feelings, but I had to admit the gesture had an effect on me. With so much going on, and barely being able to just sit and breathe most days... Yeah, to be thought about was a nice thing.

When I entered the restaurant, Sarah, the owner's daughter, greeted me. "Hey, Regina. Dine-in or to go?"

"I'm actually meeting someone."

Her eyes lit up and she leaned forward on the tall counter. "Oh, would it be the tall cutie that requested the back booth?"

She glanced over her shoulder and "the tall cutie" stood and raised his arm to catch my attention.

"Thanks, Sarah."

I gripped my purse strap and made my way to him. If my escapades at the firehouse hadn't made the town gossip mill, Regina Parker out with a man would. Alec was messing up my system of keeping my rendezvous outside the city and county lines.

A small twinge of guilt hit me thinking about word getting back to the man who I still considered my father-in-law. It'd been the same bit of worry I'd had the afternoon I'd walked out of the firehouse. Was it irrational to think he'd expect me to never move on? Probably. But holding on to that ideal had helped me over the years.

I shook off the thought. This was just lunch and only lunch. Even if my companion was a man who'd given me the best dicking down I'd had in a while. I ignored the swarm of butterflies that took up space in my stomach. I was too old and had too much shit on my plate to be reacting like some teenage schoolgirl whose crush happened to glance in her direction.

Alec placed a hand on my waist and planted a polite kiss on my cheek. "Not the greeting I want to give you, but it'll have to do," he whispered. His signature troublemaking grin made an appearance.

I ignored the ramped-up flutters and settled into the two-seater booth directly across from him. Gray wasn't a color I typically liked, but his rich, dark complexion did it wonders. When he folded his arms on top of the well-worn lacquered table his muscles flexed beneath the short-sleeve button-down. Yeah, gray definitely worked well on him.

"Much longer and I was going to think you stood me up."

"Oh, please, I'm not that late. But I do apologize for making you wait." I was, however, not about to tell him why I was late. He didn't need the strokes to his ego.

He licked his lips, and his dimples pierced his cheeks. "Some things are worth waiting for."

Sarah approached and gave me another conspirator smile before taking our drink order. The gossip network would be hearing about this for sure.

"What was all that about?" he asked after she walked off.

"What?"

"There was some exchange between the two of you."

"Oh, you mean like whatever was going on this morning?"

Alec leaned back against the red vinyl booth and ran his hand over his mouth. "Are we sharing a pizza, or would you like something else?"

Sarah returned with our drinks just as I was about to call him on the change of subject. I knew I wasn't crazy this morning, but I'd get it out of Cynthia later.

"You folks ready to order?"

Alec tilted his head toward me. "Ladies first."

"Anything you don't like on your pizza?"

"Pineapples and anchovies."

After placing my standard order for their specialty Blanco Margherita, Sarah left us alone and Alec picked right back where we'd left off.

"It must be a small-town thing."

I took a sip of my sweet tea, letting the cool liquid coat my dry mouth. "What is?"

"The silent communication. Are you two talking shit about me with grins and arched eyebrows?"

I covered my mouth to keep from spewing tea across the table over his absurd statement.

Yanking two napkins from the table dispenser, I wiped off my hand while keeping my gaze on him. "My, my, Special Investigator. I didn't take you for the fragile ego type. Or are you worried I'm going to turn you into the Wicker Man?"

This time he laughed, and I had to admit I liked the sound of it. Deep. Warm. Genuine.

"Anything's possible. I've never been to a place quite like this."

I picked up one of the breadsticks and noticed she'd left the plain kind instead of the garlic buttery ones I loved. I popped a piece into my mouth and couldn't decide if I was annoyed or amused by her assumption.

"Like what?"

"Where everybody knows everybody. Don't you wish for some privacy? Some anonymity?"

I raise one shoulder. "Been here my whole life." I chewed another piece of bread.

There had been times where I'd wished for the anonymity he spoke of. Where I'd wanted to be alone in my grief without the whole damn town offering their sympathies whenever they saw me.

"I suppose you take the good with the bad. What about you? Which highfalutin city do you hail from?"

"Atlanta born and raised. I thought the pace of Savannah was slow, but here—no offense—I'm not sure I could handle full time in a town like this. I need night clubs, places that are twenty-four hours should I want something to eat at two a.m. Action."

"No offense taken. Can't get mad at you speaking your truth. Some folks thrive on the hustle and bustle, others don't." I took a sip of my tea. "And don't knock it too hard. Places like Madison are hidden gems. Full of surprises if you know where to look."

His dark eyes bore into me. "We agree there."

Our pizza arrived, breaking the moment. The delicious smell made my mouth water and stomach growl. Silence engulfed us as we consumed our meal, but the ease of conversation returned. Over slices, I managed to learn he was one of three, and oldest by three whole minutes. He'd even puffed out his chest with pride at his proclamation. The knowledge that there was an exact replica of him out in the world was a shocker. One Alec was enough, but two? That was just plain unfair.

When he whipped out his phone to show off pictures of his adorable three-year-old niece, his demeanor changed. His eyes softened, and total sweetness and admiration colored his tone when he talked about how she had him wrapped around her little finger. All of it made my body warm, and my long-retired ovaries had a moment of confusion. I was too old to be birthing any new babies, but the man in front of me, with the way he talked about that little girl, certainly could be daddy potential for someone. Just not me.

"Were you two kind to your baby sister?"

A playful expression lit up his face. "What'd be the fun in that? But she's a lawyer now, so I'd like to think Terrance and I prepared her for the tough battles." He joked, but it was crystal clear to see how proud he was of his sister.

There was another side to Alec Hodge. Behind the jokes and the flirting was a good man. A man who loved his family and had no issue boasting about their accomplishments, telling anyone willing to listen about their greatness.

It'd been a long while since I'd spent so much time getting to know someone new. Really getting to know them. This wasn't the frivolous conversations I'd perfected to get through the sometimes awkward "date" before my companion and I got to the part of the night we were really there for.

No, sitting across from Alec shooting the breeze was nothing like that, and it was the distraction I needed. I didn't have to think and worry. He had no expectations of me or needs I had to fill. Instead, I had good, easy company as the topics meandered from one thing to another. No thought, no pretense, no struggling to fill the void before moving on to the next thing.

The ringing of my phone interrupted the peace. Seeing the time above Cynthia's flashing number let me know just how long we'd been talking. Our lunch had moved into dinner territory.

"Are you driving back tonight?" I asked as I sent her call to voicemail.

"Is that your polite way of sending me on my way again?" he replied, dodging my question.

I eased out of the booth and stretched, thankful none of my bones decided to pop and crack from sitting so long. "No. Just if you were planning to stay and wanted a better bed, Cynthia has three empty ones. She runs the B&B in town but doesn't get many guests during the week. And if you're nice to me, I'm sure I could even get you a friends and family discount." I added with a grin.

Alec grabbed his credit card from the black vinyl folder and slid it into his wallet after scooting out of the booth. "And here I thought I've been nothing but nice to you." He looked me up and down. "And if I remember correctly, I was prepared to be... nicer, but you left me." There was something in his tone as he held my gaze. A hint of accusation maybe? Wounded ego?

I swallowed down the uncertainty, grabbed my purse, and headed out of Vito's, waving bye to Sarah, with Alec trailing behind me.

❧ 12 ❧

ALEC

I TURNED ONTO THE PRIVATE DRIVE OF THE BLUE BIRD INN, the place I'd be crashing for the night, and it opened to a picturesque setting. Spending the night away from Regina wasn't exactly my plan, not that I'd had one. But I'd be lying if I said I hadn't been hopeful.

Though, the fact she insisted on being my tour guide meant the possibility wasn't entirely dead. Maybe she wouldn't be so quick to ditch me. As I parked my Jeep behind her small Buick SUV on the circular gravel driveway, I wished I'd known about this option last time I'd been here. The large white Victorian house was inviting, and I had to admit that the location had to be one of those hidden gems Regina had spoken of. There wasn't another house in sight, which was both calming and a little unnerving. The only sound came from random wildlife. Birds chirping, frogs croaking... I couldn't even hear cars from the street.

"Gorgeous, isn't it?" Regina asked as she came to stand beside me.

"It is. A much better option than the firehouse. It certainly won't be a bad runner up to where I'd like to lay my head."

She turned to face me with her hands planted on her rounded hips. "And where would that be?"

I slid my hands around her waist and pulled her to me. "Next to yours."

"In that case, sorry to disappoint. I don't think we are at the sleepover level just yet, Special Investigator."

She maneuvered around me and headed up the wide porch steps. With rocking chairs at one end and a swinging bench at the other, it was easy to imagine sitting out for early morning coffee, mid-afternoon sweet tea, or an evening glass of spirit. Regina punched in the code on the keypad door lock. A soft click followed by a whirling sound, and the door opened. It was much easier getting into this house than figuring out the hang-up of her own, because there was something. I'd picked up on it the night we had dinner, again with her mood shift after we'd had sex, and just now. There was a mystery I'd like to uncover.

Inside, the cool air was welcome after being out in the hot September weather. Georgia heat was always brutal, but the closer you got to the water, the more the humidity amped up, and it could be unbearable sometimes. Even with it being later in the day.

The large foyer had nice dark wood paneling, gleaming hardwood floors, and many more details I didn't care much about, but after years of watching home and garden shows with my mother, I'd picked up a thing or two to know the B&B was something she would probably love. I made a mental note to tell her about it since she and Dad were always looking for fun little getaways, and they'd probably like a place like Madison Island.

Regina walked over to a cabinet placed on the wall and pulled a set of keys free. "These will get you into your room. You'll be staying in the Hummingbird suite. Unfortunately, you'll only be getting a bed, no breakfast. But I do believe there are some things in the kitchen. However, this will definitely be a self-serve thing."

"Will Cynthia and Marcel be coming back tonight?"

I didn't know a lot about bed and breakfast places, but I did know that the caretakers usually lived on site, which could make things a little awkward if they didn't have thick and well sound-proofed walls since I was hoping to convince Miss Parker to at least stay with me for a little while.

Regina shook her head. "Oh, no, they don't live here. They stay in town and only use the owner's suite, which is up on the third story, for when she has guests to attend to. You have the whole house to yourself tonight, Special Investigator."

I was really starting to enjoy how she used my job title instead of my name. I think it was the emphasis she put on the special that did it for me. Either way, each time she said it, I wanted to stand a little taller.

"You're planning on leaving me all alone out here in the middle of nowhere?"

"Is a big strapping man like you scared of the dark?"

"If I say yes, will you stay?"

A salacious smile graced her full lips. "I guess I have some time to give you the lay of the land. But first let's get you settled in your room."

The view as I walked behind her up the stairs was more than pleasant. Man, this woman had an ass on her. One I was eager to get my hands on again. We went past two doors to the final one at the end of the hall.

A carved and colorfully painted hummingbird plaque hung on the dark wood. The bird theme was throughout the inn, from the name, to the decorations, and even in the wallpaper. My mother would love this place.

Regina opened the door, then stepped to the side so I could enter. A queen-sized white wrought iron bed sat at the far end of the room. The bedding was neatly folded and placed in the middle of the mattress.

"Self-serve on making the bed, too?" I joked as I dropped my bag on the bench situated under the large window. The view wasn't terrible; it overlooked the back of the property. The deck seemed like a nice place to relax, though being that close to the marshy swamp was another story.

"She wasn't exactly expecting guests, but I'm sure you can handle it." Regina pointed toward the door beside the dresser, opposite the bed. "That's your bathroom."

I peeked inside. The stall shower with its tan tiles mixed with green glass accent ones was simple in design, but a far cry more luxurious than the gym style showers at the firehouse.

"This place is really nice. Cynthia get a lot of business?" I turned to find Regina had started making the bed.

"She's doing pretty well. Only been open a few months, but stays booked on the weekends. Does weddings and such as well in case you ever wanted to go the way of your brother and sister." As she popped open the sheet, the grin on her face was temporarily hidden by the falling fabric.

I grabbed the other end and began tucking it in place. "We don't know each other well enough for a sleepover, but you'll propose?"

The whole topic of marriage was something I normally did Olympic-style gymnastics to avoid bringing up with women. The fact I wasn't breaking out in hives and looking for the nearest emergency exit shocked the hell out of me.

Regina's laugh was magical. The kind that was infectious and made you want to join in even if you didn't know the joke.

"Didn't know you were a comedian. I'm just sayin', with the way you talk about your niece, sounds like you need one of your own. Though, guess the whole marriage isn't needed for that."

I held the pillow under my chin to work the case on. "Nope. Love her to bits, but I also love leaving her and going home to a quiet house. My mom jokes she doesn't know where she went wrong with me. But I'm more than happy being fun Uncle Alec. Nothing more."

Comforter on, pillows in place, doing something so mundane, so domestic was somehow made interesting because of the woman standing across from me. A woman whose lips were upturned in a soft smile. A woman I'd been wanting to kiss again since I'd laid eyes on her in the morning.

"There are no prying eyes, or ears around," I said, making my way to her.

Her smile got bigger, and she crossed her arms. "What does that mean?"

When she was in reach, I slipped my hands around her waist. "It means we should mess up all our hard work," I whispered, leaning down to kiss her neck.

"Is that so? You think buying me pizza gets you laid?" Regina spoke the words, but craned her neck to the side to allow me more access.

I squeezed her plump ass and pressed closer. Inhaling deeply, I took in her subtle hints of sugar and rose. An interesting combination that fit her perfectly. My dick strained behind the confines of my shorts as I remembered just how good it was to be inside her. I wanted that again, and for longer. Much fucking longer than last time.

"No." I moved a hand up until I palmed one of her large breasts. "But you did say you'd like another round if I was in town again." I nipped at her earlobe. "I'm here. You're here..." I pinched her nipple and swallowed the resulting moan when I claimed her lips.

Our tongues mingled, swirling in a hedonistic dance of lust. Regina slid her warm hands under my shirt and raked her short nails down my back.

"Is that a yes?" I asked against her lips.

"I did say that. And I'm a woman of my word."

She stepped back and pulled both shirts over her head in one smooth motion. Damn, she was sexy. Her glorious tits made my mouth water, and my fingers twitched. I'd wanted access to them the day we met and now seeing them in all their glory...my dick ached to be free. Dark-brown nipples protruded behind black lace. Nipples I wanted to suck and tease until she was begging to come.

This would not be quick and dirty. I would be taking my time tonight. Erasing the space between us, I cupped both breasts in my hands and ran my thumbs over the hard buds. "That's damn good to know," I groaned before dipping my head and closing my lips around one of the taut peaks.

Regina moaned when I flicked my tongue across her stiff nipple. Hours. I could spend hours with her and still want more.

She ran her hand over my head in small circles and gripped my shoulder with the other while arching her back. I turned my attention to the other breast. Her body was a wonderland awaiting my full exploration, and I needed her naked to accomplish that. Reluctantly, I straightened but kept my eyes on her as I reached around to unclasp her bra. The delicate material hit the floor. Her topless was damn near enough to make me weep with joy.

Presumptuous, probably, but I strolled over to my bag to retrieve the box of condoms. When I turned back, Regina was fully nude and laying on the bed. My dick twitched at the sight. I felt a little bad being happy her tragedy brought her into my life, but damn if meeting her wasn't the most exciting thing to happen to me in a long time. She was confident, sexy, proud, and didn't mince words.

"You are fucking sexy as hell." I tossed the box onto the bed and disrobed so quick I was surprised I didn't fall and bust my ass.

She had no shame in focusing her attention on my dick. And I'd be lying if I said her obvious appreciation of it wasn't one hell of a boost to my ego. Not that I needed it, but considering her apparent detachment, it helped. My focus zeroed in on the neatly trimmed triangle of light-brown curly hair and licked my lips.

"You gonna stare all night, or are you gonna put those to

use?" She leaned her head toward the condoms then looked back at my erection, smile wide.

I crawled onto the bed. "I'm going to do my damnedest to use them all." She didn't resist as I nudged her legs wider. "But first, I need to see if you taste as sweet as your cakes."

Leaning forward, I kissed her again. Soft and slow. A new exploration of her mouth as my hand wandered up to hold one of her breasts. I rolled her nipple between my thumb and fore-finger, pinching slightly. Regina moaned and dug her fingers into my arm. There was no rush for the night.

I kissed along her jaw then down her neck all the while relishing in the splendid weight of her titty in my palm. With her fully nude, I inched down her body, capturing one of her large nipples between my teeth, nipping at it softly. Regina sucked in a sharp breath, but pressed my head closer. I continued to toy with the other while flicking my tongue over the hard bud.

When I pressed my thigh against her, she gripped my leg, and slowly began gyrating my limb as I continue to suck and lavish attention to her nipples. Her low moans reverberated in my ears, but I wanted to hear her scream. And there was more of her I needed to savor. I licked and kissed my way down her luscious body, committing each curve and dip to memory, until I reached my desired destination.

I slipped my hands under her hips and inhaled, drinking in her light heady scent. Her pussy glistened, wet and inviting. My mouth watered. With a squeeze to her plump ass, I finally tasted her, letting her arousal coat the tip of my tongue. Better than I imagined.

My drive to have this woman writhing and hollering out my name speared me forward. Spreading her wide, I circled the fleshy nub, which had her groaning out a low fuck. My dick throbbed at the sound, and I felt a trickle run down the head. I dipped my chin, then licked her slit from top to bottom before penetrating her as far as I could with my tongue. She grasped the back of my head and wrapped her legs around my shoulders, locking her ankles.

"Oh, god, yes, right there," she moaned.

I closed my lips around her clit and inserted two fingers in her slick opening, hooking them. I stroked and sucked, drinking in her essence while teasing her closer to the end. Her pillowy thighs cradled my head like cushions from heaven. I had one goal, and one goal only, to have this beautifully sexy woman completely fall apart at my doing.

Regina wasn't shy about taking what she wanted. She held my head and rocked against me, fucking my face until her body went rigid. As her pussy clenched then quivered around my digits, I glanced up to see her back arched and mouth open. Fuck she was beautiful. Continuing to move my fingers in and out of her body, with my other hand, I rubbed her sensitive nub. She grabbed at her large breasts, pulling at her nipples as her body began to shake.

Damn, I could have stayed between her legs all night, but my dick ached to be inside her. I kissed the inside of her thigh while reaching for the condoms. Her chest rose and fell with heavy breaths as I settled on top of her after rolling on the thin latex. I hooked one of her legs around my waist and pushed forward. Squeezing one of her magnificent tits, I closed my lips around her stiff nipple as I pulled out and thrust in again. Between Regina's sharp intakes of breath, her clenching around my dick, and the way she gripped my shoulders, I worried I wouldn't last as long as I wanted.

The headboard banged against the wall as our bodies rocked together.

With each thrust, I tried to go deeper than the last. She dug her fingers into my ass, almost pushing me in while tilting her hips. Rising to my knees, I maneuvered us, so her legs were straight in the air against my chest. Leaning forward slightly, I gripped the headboard and went to work. I pounded into her, my balls slapping against her ass as the rocking intensified, adding to the symphony of our grunts and groans. The scent of her lingered under my nose, and I licked my lips, tasting her once again. My heart beat faster. I had something to prove...I needed to leave a mark, an impression, on this woman who'd walked out on me.

"Don't stop...fuck...like that..." She dug her fingers into my forearms, and more cussing poured from her lips.

Sweat covered our bodies, the scent of sex mingled in the air, and the feel of her pussy quivering with her release acted as a jolt of electricity, fueling me to push more. I pulled out and flipped her onto her stomach. Her face was planted on the bed, but her gloriously fat ass was high in the air. I couldn't resist smacking it.

"Oh, yeah. One more time, baby," she moaned, and I obliged, spanking the other cheek.

She hissed and arched her back. I rubbed my dick across her wet pussy, teasing her before I pushed back in nice and slow, groaning deep from the back of my throat. Squeezing her ass, I moved in and out, making each stroke count. Regina gripped the headboard and rocked back and forth, slapping her ass against me.

"You look damn good ridin' my dick." I stopped moving and momentarily enjoyed the view. The way her ass jiggled with each impact. I couldn't resist smacking the plump flesh again which drew another moan from her. I reached around to fondle her clit as I once again began moving. "Who's making this pussy feel good, huh?"

When she didn't respond, I pulled out then thrust forward hard.

"Fuck! Yes, Alec. Give it to me."

Abandoning her clit, I grabbed her shoulder with one hand and gripped her waist with the other. I pumped my hips, grinding against her as I gave her what she wanted. Our grunts and groans intensified. The bed squeaked under the pressure, the banging of the headboard against the wall was a rhythmic drum that kept our tempo. Sweat trickled down my back.

With both hands, Regina held onto the wrought iron, arched her back, and cried out as another orgasm hit her. The clenching of her walls around my dick made my balls tighten. My stomach clenched and I thrust forward hard, digging my fingers into her flesh as my load shot into the condom. After a few seconds, I eased out of her and collapsed onto the bed.

"Good thing this place is empty, or our neighbors might have complained," I said, still trying to catch my breath.

She didn't speak, but huffed an airy laugh and nodded in agreement. I placed a quick kiss to her shoulder then pushed off the bed and headed to the bathroom. When I returned, Regina was buttoning her jeans. The simple act was once again a giant shot to my ego. I absolutely expected her to be in a sex stupor, still laying on the bed, gloriously naked and staring in a daze at the ceiling. I was losing my damn touch or something because this shit made no sense.

"Damn, it's like that. Again?"

She smiled at me. "Don't take it personal, Special Investigator. I got an early morning. Those pastries aren't gonna bake themselves." She grabbed her bag then strolled over to me, stretching up on her toes for a quick kiss. "There might be a few beers in the fridge downstairs. Have one, sit out on the deck, and enjoy the rest of your night."

I wrapped my fingers around her wrist when she started to walk away. "It'd be nice if you didn't keep running out on me."

"I told you it's nothing personal."

"It sure feels personal."

She turned to fully face me. "It's not. If I were to stay here any later that means I'd be dipping out in the middle of the night so I can make the drive home, maybe try to get a little more shut eye. But more than likely drinking a shit ton more coffee so I can do what I need before opening my pop-up shop. So, not about you, Alec. I got business to handle."

My shoulders sagged, and I let out a defeated sigh. "You're right. Go. Hope you get some sleep, and I'll stop by on my way out of town tomorrow." I tilted her chin for another parting kiss.

This normally would be my ideal situation. No strings in sight sex, but her damn near flipping the script on me was playing with my head. I actually wanted her to want to stay. And I had no idea how to handle that truth.

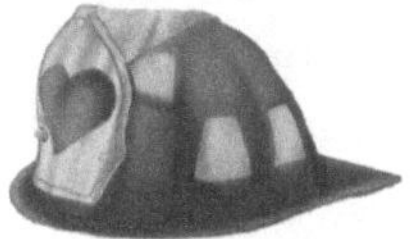

REGINA

I STIFLED A YAWN AS I HEADED TOWARD THE TRAILER MARCEL had loaned me. Having it made this whole process a little easier since I didn't have to worry about bringing the tables and tent back and forth.

"What, or should I say who, kept you up last night?"

I turned to find Cynthia grinning like a loon at me. "Girl, I think that man was on a mission to put my damn hip out or something. But it was worth it." I grabbed my side and fake hobbled the rest of the way while we both cackled.

She thought I was joking, but only partly because Alec had seemed like he was on a mission, almost as if he had something to prove. No idea why, but I was not going to turn my nose up at a good fuck.

"I'm surprised he didn't come with you then this morning, or is he already on his way back home?"

We wrestled with getting the heavy tent out of the trailer and carried it in tandem to where we would set it up.

"I have no idea."

"How do you not know? Didn't you see him this morning before you left?"

I frowned at her and set the tent down with a thud. "I left

his ass last night and went home. Had to be up too damn early. Plus, you know better. Spending the night implies a whole different set of expectations."

Cynthia shook her head. "For a woman that was so gung-ho for me to get back to dating Marcel, I can't believe you're still so anti-relationship."

We worked the covering into standing position then each grabbed a corner to walk it open.

"I'm not anti-relationship. They're great. For people who want them and have time. I don't. I have Darnell, the business, now this mess. I'm getting just what I need."

"Uh-huh. Darnell is damn near grown. Before all this crap with Trent, the business was running itself. Those tired excuses you have won't last forever."

"Not excuses. The truth. You know how much work it takes to deal with someone else all the damn time. I can't do it right now."

I swiped at my forehead, already sweating and all we'd done was get the tent set up. I knew Nick would be here shortly and it'd be just the three of us since I'd told Momma to stay home and rest. She fussed about that, but even she knew these were not the same working conditions and she didn't need to be pushing herself.

"You been saying that for years." My friend shot me a pointed stare, which I chose to ignore, and headed back to get the tables.

"Doesn't matter. Alec and I both know what's up, and we're good."

I might have been a little set in my ways, but I had a good thing going. I hadn't set out to never date again. Initially, I was simply wrapped up in my grief while trying to be both mother and father to Darnell and run the business. Time could be funny when you're so focused on one thing. My life worked for me, and I had no risk of any more heartbreak. Besides, it wasn't fair to any man that they had big shoes to fill without them even knowing it.

Alec was a timely distraction. Nothing more. Regardless of his deep-brown eyes that were begging me to stay last night. It'd been the same forlorn expression he'd had after our first hookup. I chalked it up to him wanting all the loving he could get in the short time he was here. I wasn't opposed to that, long as things stayed on my invisible terms.

Most of my gentlemen suitors were thankful for the zero strings, and I'd thought Alec gave off those same vibes, but he was making me question it. I shook off the thought. I had no time to let Special Investigator Hodge take up more of my mental space.

The sound of an engine being shut off followed by a door slamming wasn't unexpected. However, when I peeked around the trailer door, the man walking toward us with an easy gait, twirling his keys on his finger knocked me for a loop. We'd talked him up.

"Good morning, ladies. Need some help?"

"Yes, please."

"What are you doing here?"

Cynthia and I spoke at the same time. He smiled and took the table from our hands, easily carrying it to the tent and proceeded to set it up.

"I take it you didn't know he was coming?" she whispered as she grabbed two chairs.

Alec came strolling back, those perfectly white teeth and deep dimple on full display.

"You didn't answer my question."

"I came to help." He eased past me, his hard body brushing against me in an almost deliberate way as he grabbed the other table. "Cynthia, thank you for letting me stay at your place last night. It's a great spot, and I got the best sleep I've had in ages." He licked his lips and shot a glance at me.

My traitorous friend smiled large, and I somehow managed to not groan and roll my eyes.

"You're welcome. I'm glad you um...enjoyed yourself. Feel free to come back anytime."

"Thank you. I plan to come as much as I can." Alec had the nerve to wink in my direction.

Cynthia pressed her lips together but was unsuccessful in stopping her snicker. Juveniles. They were both juveniles. He walked off, and I couldn't deny how good his ass looked in the light-blue shorts he wore. The memory of how that ass clenched beneath my hands on his deep strokes zinged around my head. I flexed my fingers and diverted my gaze. It'd been a long while since a man had the ability to throw me off and steal my focus. Damn him.

"I'm just sayin', it's okay to want more now, Regina." Cynthia's words drew my attention.

"I don't."

She tilted her head, looked over at Alec, then back at me. "Time for me to dish out the same tough love you gave me a few months ago." She set down the chairs and grabbed me by the shoulders. "Stop being so damn stubborn. It doesn't have to be the sexy fire investigator, who clearly has a major thing for you, but let someone in."

I opened my mouth to protest but she shook her head.

"Losing Lawrence hurt. More than hurt. I was there, and still can't imagine that level of devastation. You are strong, fiercely independent, and you don't let shit stop you. I mean, look at what you're doing and have been doing to keep the bakery going." She paused and took a breath. "You're also scared, and that I get. But you have a lot of love to give, Regina. Quit letting the past dictate your future."

"You think I'm ready to ride off into the sunset with that man because he showed up here today?" *Showed up period. He'd come back for the sole intention of seeing me...* And it was because he'd come to simply see me that I'd left when I had last night. Alec's considerate side, and the fact I genuinely enjoyed his company had me being pulled toward a dangerous line of comfort. I'd almost been tempted to stay with him.

She picked up the chairs and a rueful smile graced her lips. "Nope. If you're happy, truly happy with the superficial, itch scratching, then I'll mind my business and let you be. But...if not, then all I'm saying is stop ruling out the possibility at the first step." She pressed her cheek to mine and air kissed me.

Alec met her halfway, took the chairs from her, and laughed at something she said. Damn him. And damn her for good measure. She knew how I like to get down, but now she wanted to throw in all these added complications of what-ifs. And him... yesterday he'd already made me start questioning things simply by showing up to check on me and now here he was to help, to work and support what I was doing, and for what gain?

I closed the doors of the trailer and looked toward my damaged shop. The ache that hit me every morning made me rub my chest. I didn't have time for the nonsense Cynthia was shoveling, and I had no energy to give to Alec. Not in the way she suggested.

"Anything else?"

I closed my eyes at the deep rumble of his voice. And was irked at myself because hearing it made the weight on my shoulders just a little lighter.

I took in a cleansing breath before answering. "Just the pastries and stuff, but..." I took a peek around his sleek body to see Cynthia and Nick already unloading my car. "Looks like they have it."

He stepped closer, invading my space. "Are you annoyed I'm here?"

My eyes went to the opening of his shirt. The colorful, geometric button-down with the two top buttons undone beckoned me to push the fabric to the side and kiss the warm, dark skin beneath it. His entire body was silky smooth save for his calloused hands. I shivered at the memory of how they'd teased me last night.

"If I was annoyed, I'd say so."

He shoved his hands into his pockets. "You don't seem all that thrilled either way. I thought I was doing a nice thing by showing up to help."

I raised my chin to look at him. His eyes were hidden behind the mirrored shades, but his brows were drawn together.

"Are you trying to earn brownie points or brownies?"

"I can't just want to be here?" The annoyance he'd questioned me on slipped into his tone.

"I suppose. But you better be ready to work, not just stare at my tits and ass all day."

Fuck if his panty obliterating smile didn't shine full force. "I'm not getting paid; I need to have some perks."

I said nothing but couldn't stop the smile his comment brought to my face. For kicks, I handed him one of the bright pink aprons, fully expecting him to balk at wearing it, but his ass wore it with pride. Cassie, Nick's sister and my newest hire before the fire, was more than happy to have Alec as her "trainee," making sure he handed out the right boxes for the orders. I could tell the gossip network had been in full swing thanks to Sarah, because as a few of the ladies came up, they gave me big smiles before spending more time than needed chit chatting with tall, dark, and sexy.

While I tried to keep my attention on the customers, every time I heard his laugh, I couldn't stop my head from turning. Damn him straight to hell.

"Now I get it," Chief Morris commented as he held out bills to me.

"Get what?"

He turned his head toward Alec. "What brought him back to town."

My body heat rising had nothing to do with the quickly climbing temperatures. What the hell was going on? How was my private life suddenly tattooed on my forehead?

"I didn't call him back. I assumed you did when he showed up."

"When who showed up?"

I startled at the voice that came from behind. I turned to see Pops. The sheriff's office was walking distance, like most places in town, and he typically cut through the square to pick up a cup of coffee for himself and an apple fritter for Ms. Lucille.

He leaned to kiss my cheek before greeting the other man. "Mornin', Pat. Who we talkin' 'bout?"

Chief scratched at his thick white beard. "That investigator I had come down due to the fire."

Pops' bushy eyebrows shot up, and he quickly scanned the area and zeroed in on the one person that didn't belong. "Is there new information? Something else happen?"

"Calm down. Don't go working yourself into a tizzy. He said it was to follow up."

The chief laughed then coughed to cover it up. I shot him a look, and a moment of mortification hit me that maybe, just maybe what happened in the firehouse, in what I considered to be his firehouse had gotten back to him. *Shit.* Alec had me fucking up. The looks and giggles were exactly why I kept my sexcapades out of town.

"Am I missing something?"

"No. Chief's just choking on his doughnut."

Chief Morris cleared his throat and winked as he walked away.

Pops frowned for a split second then shrugged it off. "Right… anyway, this is good timing. Come introduce me, Gigi, I have some questions."

The idea of introducing the man I'd spent the night having sex with to my father-in-law dropped a cement weight in my stomach. I was a grown woman, free to do what and who I wanted; I'd just always chosen to do it away from home. But I only had one sized panties, big girl ones, so I plastered a smile on my face. Cynthia placed a hand on my arm as I passed by her.

"Hey, Alec you got a moment," I called out to get his attention.

He excused himself from his fan club and did a little jog walk over to where we stood.

"What's up?" He looked from me to Pops and back to me again, the relaxed expression transitioning into a more serious look.

"This is Sheriff Parker. He's heading up the investigation. Well, more like overseeing. Either way, he wanted to talk to you."

At the mention of Pops' name, Alec's eyebrows drew together then shot up to his hairline. He stuck his hand out. "Nice to meet you, sir."

Pops grasped the extended appendage and gave a firm shake. "Same. Same. Look, when you're done here can you stop by the station? I have some questions."

"Yes, sir. I can do that."

"Good. Good, Gigi will bring you over."

Pops placed a parting kiss on my cheek and left, leaving me standing with an overly confused looking Alec.

"Your dad is the sheriff?"

I massaged my neck to loosen the tension trying to seep into my already exhausted muscles. "No. My dad is a retired postal worker who spends his days fishing, dabbling in making his own liquor, and annoying my momma. That was my father-in-law."

I could almost see him trying to work out the information I'd just supplied. The frown, the way his brow scrunched as he looked at me, and in the direction where Pops retreated and back to me again.

"No, I'm not having an affair. That's not the kind of person I am. I am a widow, and that's all I'll say on the subject."

The familiar pang twisted in my gut. I hated that fucking word. I turned on my heel and headed back to my station. I didn't want to or need to see the pity and sympathy that undoubtedly would start to fill his eyes. I'd dealt with that look for far too long.

❧ 14 ❧

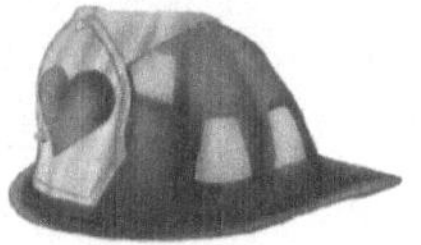

ALEC

For the remaining few hours, I kept stealing glances at Regina. So many questions circled like buzzards in my mind. A widow. And she didn't want to speak about it, but I needed to know. How long ago? Was I the first man she'd been with since? If so, did I want to shoulder that sort of emotional responsibility?

By the time we broke down everything and locked up, I was conflicted on how I wanted to proceed. Yes, I enjoyed her company, and the sex was amazing, but did I really want to be tangled up if she got attached? I laughed at myself. Regina Parker attached? The very woman that promptly left me after sex. Twice. The very woman I'd spent my cherished off days coming to see because she left me right after sex. And I'd showed up to work in the hot-ass sun to help her. That woman didn't get attached, but she somehow had my ass jumping through hoops.

"Can I get in on the joke?" Regina came sauntering over after saying her goodbyes to her friend.

I pushed off my Jeep and waved to Cynthia as she climbed into her truck. "Just thinking."

Regina raised one brow, but said nothing. She placed her

hands on her lower back and stretched while groaning out the change of subject. "It's about a ten-minute walk to the sheriff's station, or like a two-minute drive. Pick your poison."

A sheen covered her forehead, and the wrap she wore to keep her locs up was darker where it touched her skin from the sweat. I had no idea how early she had to get up to do all the baking, then get it over here before people showed up, but the amazing woman in front of me had put in a full day's work before noon.

I hit my key fob; the lights flashed, and the locks popped. "Your chariot awaits." I opened the door with flourish.

She laughed but used the hand grip to hoist herself into the hot car. Damn, I should have had the AC running already. The song that came blaring out of the speakers was about deep throating and I quickly turned it down and apologized. She laughed and shook her head. "No need to apologize, Special Investigator. It ain't something I'm opposed to."

Nope, nope, nope. I would not let my mind wander to the thought of her full lips wrapped around my dick. Not while we were about to go sit with her father-in-law. I cleared my throat and attempted to force the idea away as I cranked up the air. "It should cool off in a bit."

She looked over at me. "You know you can take that off."

I glanced down at the pink apron I still wore. "I don't know. I kinda like it."

She reached forward and turned the vents so the air hit her directly in the face. "Translation, the pocket is full of all the numbers you collected today."

I turned so my back pressed against the door. "Wrong. None were offered up, and if they had been, I wouldn't have taken them." I put my Jeep in reverse. "I have the only one I want."

"Whatever you say, Special Investigator." Regina leaned her head back on the seat and closed her eyes. "Out of the parking lot take a left. At the second stoplight, take another left. The station will be on the right."

Wasn't going to lie, some of the women who flirted with me

today were cute, including the one I spent most of the day working with, but that would be messy. Messing with two women in a bigger city could be enough of a headache, but in this small ass town... That was asking for trouble. I glanced over at my resting passenger. Besides, I wouldn't want to cause Regina any drama.

The station was a nondescript brown brick building. The only thing indicating it was the right place was a simple sign at the entrance of the small parking lot. As I pulled into a space, an unusual set of nerves overcame me. Sure, I'd met her mother. She was an interesting woman, not the typical, or what I would expect to be a typical mom, with her lack of a filter and ease of calling me out with barely knowing me. But the man we were about to go see, even though he wasn't her father—whom I'd yet to meet still—the sheriff was clearly someone important in her life, and it had been a long time since I'd had to deal with the families of any of the women I'd slept with. Things never progressed to that point, and I liked it that way. I took off the apron and let out a slow exhale in an attempt to get my shit together.

Inside, the few officers milling about greeted us as we passed by. Some were all smiles toward Regina, and others watched me under a suspicious gaze. Regina made a beeline to the back of the building toward the office where the door was half open. She smiled at the older light-skinned woman sitting at the desk right outside whose silver hair was pulled up in a neat bun. The glasses perched on the end of her wide nose were secured with a beaded chain. She fit every stereotypical image of the grandmotherly librarian., Regina quickly introduced me to the woman, Ms. Lucille, then knocked lightly before peeking her head in while pushing the door wider.

"Gigi, how was it today?" The sheriff greeted while waving us in.

He appeared less imposing sitting behind his large wooden desk. For a man I suspected had to be pushing in on seventy, you wouldn't be able to tell it from first glance. His salt and pepper hair was whiter at the sideburns. Worry lines creased his forehead and around his mouth, giving him the appearance of always being deep in thought.

"Same as has been. We sold out, so something, but it's not the numbers I'm used to, so the sooner we put this to bed, the sooner I can get to reconstructing and back to real business."

"I know. We're working on it."

Regina settled into one of the chairs opposite the desk, and I took the other one.

I wiped my sweaty palms on the front of my shorts and made eye contact with the gentleman across from me. My nerves would stay on the inside, and I would keep this professional. "Sheriff Parker, you said you had a few questions for me?"

He shifted a few papers around before coming up with the red file, then proceeded to go through it a few moments before he finally found what he was looking for. "Yes, yes, here we are. With us having a suspect in mind, I just need to clarify some things on your report."

A suspect? I shot a quick glance toward Regina, who sat unfazed by that news, then back at the sheriff. "Sure, I can help as best I can. What do you need to know?"

"I just want to verify that we think his intention was only to do property damage not to hurt anyone."

"Pops! He's not that reckless. I mean, he did it well after the shop was closed. And it's not like where I live is a secret. If he was tryin' to hurt me, he knows where to find me."

They had some secret exchange, with the sheriff's nostrils flaring before his thick brows cinched together. Regina, however, wasn't going to back down. I wanted her to back down. Hell, I wanted the sheriff to offer up some sort of police protection. How in the hell could she be so nonchalant about the possibility of this man—whoever the fuck he was—maybe showing up to do physical harm to her?

But it wasn't my place. Despite of how easily we got along,

and how much I truly enjoyed her company, the fact remained that Regina and I were barely able to be considered friends so, I bit my tongue and reminded myself it wasn't my place regardless of how pissed it made me.

She straightened in her chair and stared directly at the older man. "He's a thief and now possibly an arsonist, but we don't know for sure it was him. Regardless, I don't see Trent as being something any more sinister. If it was him, I don't think he was tryin' to kill me or anything like that."

Trent? Now I had a name to go with the asshole who'd put her in this predicament. And thief? So, this was not out of the blue or fucking random. There was a reason why he'd done what he'd done other than just being a class A dip shit.

The sheriff relented, closed the file, and rested his forearms on his desk. "You say that, but honestly, you didn't expect the man to swindle money from you. And yes, right now it's only suspicions he was behind the fire, but I'm fairly damn certain both our guts are right. Because the man there says arson, so who else would do such a thing?"

Both parties looked to me as if I were privy to information I probably shouldn't hear, but they'd invited me here and started on this conversation, so it wasn't like I was eavesdropping.

"Do you two want me to step outside?" Not that I wanted to, but if this was going to be a private conversation between them the courteous thing would be to leave.

Regina sighed and rolled her neck from side to side a few times before finally shaking her head. "Nah, you can stay, it's fine. You're right, Pops, and I get it. I guess despite all the shit Trent's done I don't want to believe he'd do anything worse. Maybe that makes me a naive fool, but that's where we are. Doesn't matter, though. He did what he did, and he needs to answer for it. So, did you find him?"

The sheriff leaned back in his chair, and his shoulders hunched over just a bit. I didn't know the man, but from the look on his face the news he was about to say couldn't be good.

"Sorry to say, but it seems like Trent done jumped bail."

"What? What the fuck, I thought he was in Augusta."

"Yeah, that's what was on the bail release form, but we called and had the Augusta PD check in with his folks, who he's supposed to be staying with. They said he left, and they claim they don't know where. Which only adds to my suspicions. Why run now?"

"No good sneaky bastard."

My own temper rose as I listened. "Sheriff, do you think he'd show up here and try to do something to her?" I attempted to keep my tone calm and neutral.

The man had committed one crime, gotten bail, committed a second and now he was in the wind. These small-town people seemed to have an easy-going outlook on life, but this, to me, demanded a bit more urgency.

The sheriff sucked his teeth and stared at me for a long while before he set his attention on Regina. I could worry about whatever suspicions he might have over my concerns later; my priority was on making sure nothing happened to the stubborn woman sitting to my left. And if I was right about her status not only in this town, but with the man tasked with keeping all the residents safe, it would be his as well. And that tracked with why he'd asked me here in the first place.

"Gigi, I'm gonna be making sure extra patrols pass by your house."

"I don't need that."

"Like hell," I countered. "You said this man knows where you live, and he's already had violent tendencies toward you."

Both of them stared at me. The sheriff tilted his head and chuckled. Regina's eyes were slits, and her lips pulled into a deep frown. I'd overstepped, just like the first morning I'd found her setting up shop in the parking lot. And she could and probably would get in my ass about it in the car. But she was already dealing with the aftermath of an apparent betrayal of epic proportions. She didn't need to be taking her safety so lax. What was wrong with this stubborn woman?

To burn down her place seemed personal. Really personal. I shot another glance at her. I couldn't stop my mind from wandering and being jealous. Had there been something more between her and the Trent guy? It was the wrong time to be worried about such things, but I couldn't help it. There had to be a reason. Some reason that he would resort to something so extreme to get back at her and spurned lover was the first thing that popped in my mind. Which made the threat of him returning even more dire.

I had no claim to her. What we had was casual at best—if even that. But if that fucker had destroyed her business because she'd gotten what she needed and told him no... The protective side of me wanted to find him and beat his ass for the trouble he'd caused.

The sheriff assured Regina they were on it and working closely with the Augusta Police Department. They had already let Trent's parents know that if he wasn't found soon, he forfeited his bail and that they could lose their house since it had been put up for collateral. Silently, I hoped that would be enough incentive for them to track down their weasel of a son and get his ass back here to answer for what he'd done.

"Want lunch?" I asked once we were back in my Jeep.

The weariness that had been on her face on the ride over was nothing compared to the additional stress she seemed to be shouldering now. And just like when I'd rolled my ass out of bed bright and early in the morning, I wanted to do something, anything to siphon off some of that stress.

I didn't know the full story, and maybe she'd tell me. Part of me hoped she would. Yes, she had the whole town around her, supporting her, but there was something about her that led me to believe she was holding it down on her own. Or trying to, anyway. However, from what little I did know, Regina had a lot on her plate between whatever the first crime was and now the fire. She was a woman trying to keep her head above water. Even if she wanted to pretend otherwise.

"Imma have to take a rain check on that today, Alec. I really just need to go home, shower, and just be." The last word was delivered with a heavy sigh.

It was still a brush-off, but I didn't take it as personal as the one from last night or the first one. But I also couldn't leave her in such a somber mood. That didn't sit right with me.

"Rain check it is. And you know I'll come collect." I grinned and cast a quick glance over at her, happy to see that her lips were upturned into a soft smile.

"I'm sure you will, Special Investigator. I'm sure you will."

We rode the rest of the short distance back to her bakery in silence, and although I wasn't quite ready to leave her yet, I understood that she wanted her time and space alone after the news she'd received today. It wasn't about me.

I whipped into the spot next to her small SUV but didn't kill my engine because it was too damn hot to be without AC. I threw it in neutral and pulled up the emergency brake, then turned to face her. What she was doing for now worked, but there had to be a better option. "You know, working with you today got me thinking. Have you ever considered a food truck?"

"No need in a place this small. Everyone knows where to find me."

"Yeah, I get that, but hear me out. It would make sense because you don't know how long it's going to take to rebuild, and in the interim, if you're going to keep doing these morning sales, having the truck might work out a little bit better for you. You could customize it and cook more so you wouldn't sell out as fast."

Skepticism showed on her face, but I kept going to sell her on the idea before she could shoot me down.

"Plus, food truck festivals are a thing. You could take the show on the road. Have your main thing here and then later, once you're back up and running, do a couple of the festivals.

The first day I caught you out here, you said you had people depending on you, a business to run. This would be an increase, right?"

The more I thought about it, the more it made sense. To me at least. I'd attended my fair share of foodie festivals, and the sweets trucks always were a hit. I had no doubt Regina would make a killing.

She leaned against her door and folded her arms across her chest pushing those glorious breasts upward. "Why are you trying to be so helpful?"

"Why are you being so suspicious?"

"You barely know me, you have no skin in this game, so what's the angle?"

I tightened my hand on the steering wheel and sucked in a breath, then let it out slowly. "Is it just me, or are you this way with everyone?"

"What are you talking about."

"There is no angle, Regina. From the moment I met you, you've had this passion for your business and your employees. I don't know, maybe some of that is rubbing off on me and I just want to be a part of it as much as I can. Anyway, I'm just trying to help. I don't want anything in return." I relaxed back against my seat. "It's not like I need to butter you up to get into your pants. Been there, and I have a feeling I could be again without giving you useful suggestions." I winked at her, and she smiled again.

"Is that so?"

"Yes, yes, it is."

She shook her head and laughed. "Boy, you're a mess. An arrogant mess."

"But not wrong."

She looked me up and down, letting her gaze linger on my crotch, and her lips twitched to the side before she made eye contact with me. "But not wrong." Regina turned to open the door but stopped. "Thank you. I'm not sure I have the energy to take on what you suggested right now. But thank you for wanting to help."

Why did two little words mean so much? The sincerity in her eyes, the soft smile on her face, all of it made me want to do a victory lap.

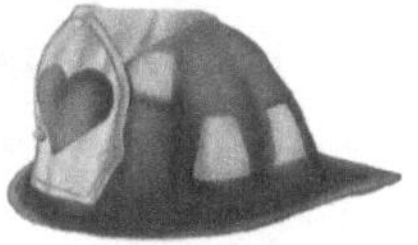

❧ 15 ❧

REGINA

I STARTED TO PUNCH IN THE DOOR CODE, BUT MARCEL'S smiling face greeted me instead.

"Hey, hey Gina." He gave me a quick hug then stepped to the side.

"Hey yourself."

"Don't worry, I'm not infringing on your ladies' night. I'll be out of y'all's hair shortly."

I lightly pushed his shoulder. "You know you want to stay. We are way more entertaining than poker."

He laughed. "Maybe, but the fellas and Remi are looking forward to making some easy cash off me. I'd hate to disappoint. Anyway, go on up, I left the door unlocked for you."

He gave me another quick hug then left. The mention of Remi brought the statement Alec had made to the forefront of my mind. A food truck. I'd brushed it off when he'd first mentioned it, but it'd stayed as a seed of an idea in the back of my thoughts for the rest of the week.

Soon as I stepped over the threshold, I took a big inhale. The subtle sage and lavender smell welcomed you in and made you feel right at home. In the parlor, one set of guests sat cozied up

93

on the sofa. I waved on my way up the two flights of stairs to the owner's suite.

"Cyn, it's me," I called out as I headed up the steps after locking the door behind me.

Marcel had done one hell of a job turning the attic of Cynthia's old Victorian into a homey and stylish one-bedroom apartment even if it didn't get as much use as she'd once planned. Though, she also hadn't planned on moving back to Madison Island or reconnecting with her old flame, and she really hadn't planned on marrying the man.

But plans change.

My stomach growled as soon as I caught wind of the garlic bread. I loved Cynthia's lasagna, and it was the comfort meal I was in desperate need of. Which was why I suspected she'd made it.

She handed me a glass of wine. "Hey, lady."

I took a long sip of the pinot and let out a long, appreciative sigh. Cynthia slid the bottle my way just as Irene reappeared on the screen.

"Alright, Gina, give me the scoop. Cyn has been filling me in a bit, but I need to know it all," she said in lieu of a greeting.

"The scoop on what?"

"Everything. The shit with Trent being MIA. When the bakery will get back up and running. And, of course, what's going on with Alec."

Cynthia handed me a plate, then picked up her tablet and we moved the party over to her comfy sectional.

I squinted at the screen. "Wait, Irene, why are your eyes all red?"

"Oh, nothing. My contacts were irritating me."

Cynthia and I glanced at each other. I didn't know how long they'd been chatting before I arrived, but the look on Cyn's face told me she didn't believe that answer. Irene wanted the scoop on me, but we needed to find out what was going on with her. However, as much as she loved being the center of attention, it always had to be on her terms, which meant she wanted all the details, but at times gave very little in return. She had a real knack for being able to simultaneously make things about her while also milking you for information. Whatever was going on would have to wait until she was ready to share. Thirty plus years of friendship had taught us that.

"Alright, Gina back to you. I got a full bottle of wine and the house to myself. I need all the deets about what's going on since I can't be there."

I refilled my glass and thought about where I wanted to start. After another long drink, I finally relayed all the information Pops had discussed earlier in the week. From the police protection to Trent being gone. As I spoke, the hollow feeling that grew each day ate away at me. I bit into the warm, gooey pasta dish and moaned my appreciation. The first taste hit the spot, plus, I needed food on my stomach stat if I was going to keep drinking.

"So, the Sheriff hasn't had any updates on Trent's location?" Cynthia asked.

I shook my head. "No, but Trent's parents are being a little more cooperative now that they know that they could lose their house with him jumping bail. They think he either went to Florida or Alabama. Pops is using his connections to see what he can do, and I just have to trust he's on it."

"It fucking sucks, Gina," Irene said, disdain colored each of her words. "Seriously, how can he do that? The fucking stealing was bad enough, but to set your place on fire and then just skip town? He should have never fucking gotten bail. I'm so pissed, and I wish I could be there."

Cynthia put down her food then wrapped her arms around my shoulders and gave me a quick hug. "We have to let the authorities do what they do. That part is out of our control. We will just have to focus on what we can do like getting up at the ass crack of dawn to help bake and to set up shop."

I laughed and hugged her back. "I appreciate you doing that

for me. I'm sure Marcel is tired of his wife leaving before he does every morning."

Cynthia rolled her eyes. "Serves him right. I've woken up alone many of mornings because he gets an early start at work. And he'll be doing the same thing once the plans are finalized and he gets to putting the bakery back together so Just a Bit of Sugar can reopen for business."

"Yeah, you're right. And Irene, don't start more this 'you're a terrible friend crap' because you aren't here. You live like four-teen hours away, not to mention you have your patients and your husband."

I wasn't sure if Cynthia caught it, but I sure did when Irene's face scrunched at the mention of her husband.

"Yeah, I know, but I should still be there. And don't even get me started on how my dad is pressuring me to come back and take over the family business. He tries the guilt trip, saying he can't retire if he doesn't leave the practice in good hands, as if Dr. Michaels hasn't worked with him for the last ten years."

"Girl, you know I get that. Look at what I do. Mabel Charles wouldn't dare leave the bakery to someone not family. Darnell has no interest, my siblings really had no interest, so thank good-ness there's Tricia. She'll be the next head of the family baking empire."

"I know you do, but before we get too sidetracked about living up to our parents' expectations, this is supposed to be fun, and I want all the hot info on your new firefighter."

Cynthia laughed quietly as she got up to retrieve a second bottle of wine after emptying the last of the current one into her glass.

"First off, he's not a firefighter, he's the fire investigator." I bit into the buttery garlic bread and savored it before continuing. "Secondly, he's not mine."

A weird feeling pinged me as I said those words. It was the same tendril of annoyance I'd had every time I saw him smiling or laughing with the female customers who were shamelessly flirting with him. Our little town didn't get too many visitors, especially not ones who looked like him. Alec Hodge was like a new attraction that everyone wanted to see. Or ride...

"Uh-huh, right and that's why that man gave up his off-days to drive down here to see you and then worked his ass off with us. You got your name all over him whether you want to admit it or not," Cynthia said as she sat back down with more pinot.

"Oh, yes, honey. Sounds like you done put it on him good," Irene added, laughing hard.

"That's the damn truth. There are dents in my damn wall."

"There are not you filthy liar!" I exclaimed.

At least I hoped there weren't, but the bed had been banging pretty hard.

"If I didn't have guests booked, I'd show your ass the proof."

My body heated. It's not like they didn't know of my sexual escapades. Hell, we'd all shared plenty of stories over the years, but being on the spot about this one seemed different.

"Anyway. He's a good time and a distraction. I don't know why you two insist on reading more into it."

"Maybe because I can see something about him makes you happy and I want that for you," Cynthia answered.

Irene moved closer to the screen. "Oh, do tell. He's not a hit it and forget it? I swear I'm missing all the good stuff."

I rolled my eyes over both their antics. "He puts it down, which lowers my stress. Nothing more. Nothing less." I stuffed more of the delicious food into my mouth. I'd be making a to-go plate for sure.

"Don't let her fool you, Irene. When he was there, she kept watching him. And, oh...the way she lit up when he appeared." Cynthia eyed me over her glass with a smug look on her face.

Damn her.

"Don't listen to the foolishness she's talking. I was surprised to see him, that was it."

"Maybe, but I think it says something. He not only came to see you again, but he also got up to work," Irene commented.

Even through the screen her eye of judgment was strong. And I had a sneaking suspicion that before I'd arrived Cynthia had filled Irene in on the conversation we'd had the morning Alec arrived to help out. Which was precisely why I wasn't going to tell them we'd had some form of communication the last couple of days. He'd taken the text I'd sent checking to make sure he'd arrived home safely as an invitation. And I hadn't bothered to correct him. Nothing much more than a basic "how's your day been," but I would not analyze how four simple words acted as the calming exhale I needed at the end of the day.

"I think y'all both need to lay off the liquor because it's got y'all fucked up thinking this is anything more. Besides, even if I was entertaining the idea of attempting a relationship—and that is a super-sized if—there is too much on my plate. I ain't got no time for more than what I'm doing." I picked up my glass and settled back against the comfortable sofa, but shot up when a thought came to mind. "Cyn, can you text Marcel for me. Ask him to check with Remi to see if she knows where I might be able to get my hands on a truck that can be converted into one of those food trucks."

"Remi?" Irene questioned. Her voice hitched at the end, spiking to a higher pitch.

"Don't start, Irene."

"Start what?"

I arched a brow and pursed my lips. "You know damn well what."

I never understood Irene's issue with Remi. We also never thought our friend to be the mean-girl type, but Irene and Remi were like oil and water with Irene taking issue with most things Remi did. I'd have thought twenty plus years later whatever the issue was would have been done, but with her reaction, I guessed I was wrong.

Irene flipped her hair over her shoulder. "I don't know what you're talking about. I just don't understand what you'd need her for." She tried to come off as dismissive, but if I wasn't mistaken, Irene had a bit of a curious lilt mixed into her question.

Cynthia was typing away on her phone and started explaining without looking up. "She's taken over her father's autobody shop, and let me tell you, that woman knows her way around an automobile. My Four Runner is purring like a kitten these days."

"Same with my little Buick. So, if anyone can do this, it would be her."

Cynthia put her phone down. "Sent. And do what exactly?"

"Yeah, what exactly?" Irene echoed.

I knew mentioning Alec again would put me promptly back in the hot seat, but these were my girls. Through ups and down, no matter how much shit we gave each other from time to time. It was a good plan, and he deserved the credit.

"Before Alec left, he mentioned that maybe I should look into getting a food truck. For now, it might be a better option for how I'm doing the morning sales, but later he said something about going to food truck festivals or such other nonsense."

I took a big gulp of my wine and willed my heart rate to get to a normal pace. It made no sense that I would be nervous to begin with, but as their silence stretched on, I had an absolute moment of doubt.

But then a large smile stretched across Cynthia's face, and she broke out in a taunting song with Irene quickly joining in.

"Regina and Alec sittin' in a tree, K-I-S-S-I-N-G..." Their torturous singing faded into deep, howling laughter.

"I can't stand either one of you heifers."

Cynthia wiped tears from her eyes. "You love us, and you know it. However, where Mr. Alec Hodge is concerned...we'll let you keep living in denial a little longer."

"Yeah, Gina. I mean a food truck is a smart idea. Here in New York, they have festivals and such all the time."

"Had them in Portland, too," Cynthia added.

"It's a solid plan. And, I mean you can't really deny if he's invested in seeing you succeed it could mean—to him at least—

this might be more than just sex," Irene said, her voice full of "I told you so" without actually speaking it.

"That's what I tried to tell her," Cynthia affirmed.

Yes, seeing and talking to Alec was enjoyable. And though I was loathed to admit it, having him take interest, to express concern, it did get past my normal barriers. Maybe it was his lack of expectations for me, or maybe it was he showed up at a weak moment of my life, or some combination. What I started to realize was despite the lies I told to myself and the denials I made to my girls, he was getting to me. And I was entirely annoyed over that fact.

❧ 16 ❧

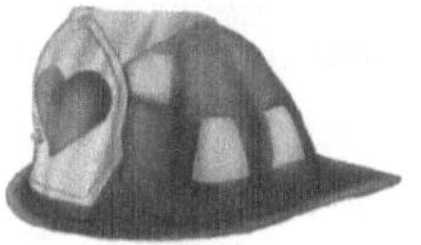

ALEC

I parked my Jeep behind my mother's Maxima and exited the car after wrestling with the oversized unicorn balloon that had been a driving hazard for the last four hours. But it'd be worth it to see the joy on Mia's face. Pink and white balloons were tied to the mailbox, and matching streamers decorated the door along with a giant sparkling four.

Juggling the gifts, I managed to get the door open to a chorus of barks from my brother and sister-in-law's two Schnauzers. The noise brought Terrance around the corner with the birthday girl right behind him. The moment she saw me, Mia became a blur of pink and shimmers as she barreled down the hall.

I managed to hand off the gifts to my brother just in time. "There's my favorite niece." I scooped her up and spun her in the air. Her infectious giggling filled the foyer.

As expected, once she laid eyes on the giant balloon, she got excited. I placed her down and made sure she was steady before I handed her the string. Off she went, running full steam back toward the kitchen yelling for her mom to see the unicorn.

"You spoil her," Terrance commented.

I shrugged. "I consider it making sure she's well-loved."

"Right. I'm surprised there isn't a pony or something outside."

"Who says there isn't?"

"Imitation me is here," Terrance announced, and I shoved his shoulder.

"I'm older, so if anyone is an imitation it's you. Remember that."

Janet, my lovely sister-in-law walked over and kissed my cheek. "When she came back in with that balloon, I figured it was you. Glad you could make it."

"You know I wouldn't miss it."

I'd had to switch my days off with Sasha, plus promise to take her kitchen duty rotation next time we worked together, but it was worth it. Terrance carried the gifts outside to where the party would take place in an hour, and I went over to greet my folks.

"She's been asking when you'd get here," Mom said.

We both looked over to where Mia played in the yard, spinning around and tugging at the string. Her tiara caught the sun each time she moved.

"Would have been here sooner, but there was an accident on the highway that added nearly forty-five minutes to my commute."

"How are things going?" Dad inquired.

They'd both thought I was a little nuts to leave a job I'd been at for almost eight years, where I'd gained some rank. They worried I was moving backward in my career and were only mildly convinced of the decision when I informed them I could eventually get out of going on calls and only do the investigations. That part they liked since from the beginning neither were fond of me choosing what they considered to be a dangerous job.

Of my siblings, I was the only one doing blue collar work, with Terrance owning his own accounting firm and Leila being an attorney. But desk jobs weren't for me. And while I was looking for the bump in pay that came with being an investigator, along with feeding the curiosity I'd always had trying to understand the how and even the why, I was nowhere near ready to give up the rush that came along with hearing the alarm go off and running off to fight a blaze.

"Slow." I headed over to the fridge and pulled out a bottle of water. "But you two need to go visit this town I was at. You'd love it."

Terrance and Janet came walking back in with Mia, who ran right over to me, still clutching her balloon.

"You two might like it as well. Take a weekend to relax, and you can even leave this troublemaker with me." I tickled her belly, which made her laugh.

"Did you just offer to babysit?" my brother asked, feigning shock.

I rolled my eyes. "Maybe not with that attitude."

"I still want that weekend. Don't let his lack of gratitude make me suffer," my sister-in-law commented, shoving her husband while laughing. "One is easier, but two..." She let the words die out but ran her hand over her stomach.

Minor chaos erupted with my mom instantly getting teary eyed as she went over to hug Janet, and we all offered up congratulations. I was excited for them. They'd had a hard time conceiving Mia and had to use IVF to be successful.

"We just found out a few days ago but wanted to share with you all since you're here," Terrance said and placed a kiss on his wife's cheek.

Mia transferred herself from my arms to her father's when I got close to give him a hug.

"Another subject for her royal highness."

"Yes. And all the more reason to take a weekend away. So, what were you saying, Alec?" Janet said, circling back to the first topic.

"Well, my first investigation assignment sent me to this small-ass town I'd never even heard of called Madison Island. It's about forty-ish minutes from Savannah. And when I say small, I mean like I don't think it takes more than ten, fifteen minutes tops to get to any one place in town small. It's nuts."

"Okay, so why are you trying to send us city people?" Terrance asked.

"It sounds quaint," Mom said, giving Dad a look that meant they were likely to go.

I pointed to our parents. "Because of that right there. Mom loves that kind of thing. Anyway, on my second trip, Regina got me the hook-up so I could stay at this B&B."

"Who's Regina?" Janet asked, with a slight grin on her face.

"She's the reason I was there."

Mom slid onto the barstool on my left, and her eyes got the same twinkle Janet's held. "Oh really?"

I knew that tone. "Not like that. She was my assignment. Well, a fire at her bakery. Besides, Terrance and Janet are giving you all the grandbabies, and I'm sure Leila will as well. You don't need me."

Mia started fussing, complaining about being hungry. I moved into the seat vacated by her father after he got up to fix her a snack.

Mom placed her warm hand on my cheek. "Oh, honey, it's not about the grandbabies, though I don't think I can have too many. It's about you finding some nice young lady to settle down with. Or are you planning on the bachelor thing forever?"

This was a talk we'd had plenty of times before. Not only did I not have the same sort of white-collar job as my siblings, I was also the only one to not be in any sort of serious, monogamous relationship. The last time I was, I'd been in my early twenties, and it hadn't worked out so well. Mainly because I'd had a hell of a hard time adapting to the monogamous part. I'd always thought myself to be a fairly good guy, but the hurt I'd caused my ex haunted me for a long time. And I'd been avoiding a repeat ever since.

"Not forever. I consider myself a late bloomer and still

sowing my oats, as they say." I shot her a playful grin, which resulted in her sighing heavily and instructing my father to "get his son." I wrapped my arm around her shoulder. "Just being honest, Mom. Besides, everyone isn't cut out for relationships. I figured it's better to recognize this fact about myself." Rather than repeat mistakes of the past. Though I kept that thought to myself.

"Don't sell yourself short, sweetie. I can feel it in my bones. There is a woman out there that will change your whole world. Just you wait."

Her prediction immediately made me think of Regina and how I responded to her, especially how she was fucking with my head in regard to her willingness to give me everything I just told my parents I was after. Her strong-willed independence. Her passion and drive even in the face of so many hurdles. She was one resilient woman, and I respected that.

Kids, those still weren't on my radar, but Regina Parker... Well, she was changing the game.

17

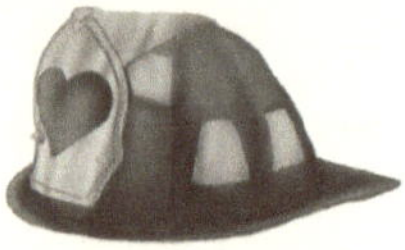

REGINA

I SANG ALONG TO WHITNEY'S "HOW WILL I KNOW" AS I drove down Main on my way to meet Remi. It'd only taken her a couple of weeks to locate a possible option. As I slowed to a stop at the red light, I squeezed the steering wheel and tried to roll some of the tension from my neck. I still couldn't believe I was possibly moving forward with this whole thing.

When I'd brought up the food truck idea, I'd expected Momma to balk at it, but she'd given me her full support, saying she trusted my judgment and it was my call. That support, however, came with a heavy dose of side eye and "I told you so" looks when she'd learned where the idea had originated. She'd been as bad as Cynthia and Irene. The man had given me one possibly helpful suggestion and they all acted like he damn near walked on water because of it.

I huffed a laugh as the light turned green. Hell, even Tricia was also on board, and she agreed with Alec on the food trucks being a big deal and that the expansion would be good for us in the long run. She'd even taken an elective course that had been offered on running a food truck. That knowledge was going to be a huge help, and it warmed my heart to know she was truly invested.

I eased into the parking lot of Martin Auto body. After parking, I picked up the cellophane bags of cookies. Snickerdoodle for Remi, they were her favorite, and mixed options for the three guys that worked for her. Gravel crunched under my feet as I made my way toward the gray brick building. It was small, with only three bays, and a little dingy, but I didn't know a person in town whose hood Remi hadn't been under.

Instead of entering through the glass door that led to the lobby, I headed to where I knew I'd find Remi—the shop area. Music blared and was nearly drowned out by the various sounds of clanks and drills as they worked.

"Hey, Ms. Parker," Tony greeted. He'd graduated the year behind Darnell and had been one of the students in Marcel's carpentry class. However, he'd been more into cars, so Marcel worked it out with Remi for him to apprentice under her.

"How are you today, Tony?" I handed off all but one of the bags to him. "Be sure to share."

Devon, one of her other employees knocked on the hood of an old Chevy. "Hey, Boss, Regina's here."

Remi peeked around the truck and acknowledged me with a nod. She pulled an oil-stained blue rag from the back pocket of her dark-blue work coveralls and wiped down the tool she'd been using before dropping it on the red and silver rolling cart beside her, then peeled the black latex gloves from her hands. "I parked it around back."

"I didn't think you'd find something so fast," I commented as I followed her around the side of the building.

"I lucked out and happened to make a few phone calls at the right time. A buddy of mine knew a guy who knew a guy. You know how it goes."

The scent of the smoker from The Shack got stronger and almost was enough to overpower the lingering motor oil aroma. Almost. But it did make my stomach growl. I would definitely be popping in for lunch once we finished up.

"Here she is," Remi proclaimed as we came to a stop in front of a robin egg blue VW. "It runs okay, made the drive here easily enough, but I can get it in tip-top shape." She opened the driver's side door.

I had no idea how she managed to talk the owner into letting her take the truck. I would have been more than willing to drive to Statesboro to see it, but she'd worked some magic for sure. Cookies weren't enough of a payment for her time and effort, but she'd refused any monetary compensation. I stepped closer to take a peek inside. The seats were upholstered in a cream vinyl with trim that matched the paint color. The space between the two front seats was open to the back.

"Climb on in. I don't know what all you need, but hopefully it's roomy enough."

"Brought these for you since you won't take my money." I handed her the cookies before I got in for a closer inspection.

"You're dealing with enough. This is me trying to help how I can."

I smiled at her. Small-town life had its downsides, but once again, the sense of community that could be found outweighed any negatives for me. Once past the seats, I was able to stand at full height. It wasn't bad, but then again, I wouldn't really know the difference.

"It's a 1960 VW Split Screen custom. The guy who owns it was going to do ice cream or something but decided he wasn't really into running a business before he even got started." Remi leaned against the back wall and crossed her arms. "Anyway, he apparently had the VW van converted and stopped there, but he did give me the name of some company that can trick it out with all the equipment you need."

It seemed spacious with two of us in the space, but that was without anything other than two stainless steel counters. Once ovens and such were installed, it could get tight. But I liked the retro look.

Could I really do this?

Better question was, did I need to be doing this now? With

so much on my plate, starting up with would almost be a second business seemed like I was adding on too much. The investment. The time. The fucking energy, of which I was running low on. I'd had to call on every favor and lean on people more than I cared to all in the name of protecting the family business and keeping it afloat. And this was for the good of the bakery. It wasn't just about me.

I let out a heavy sigh. "How much he asking?"

"He said sixty, but my buddy thinks he can get him down to fifty since it is just the shell and you gotta install everything."

I pinched the bridge of my nose. Fifty wasn't terrible. Since I'd decided to give the whole thing serious consideration, I'd been doing some online research. Checking out for-sale ads and things of that nature. We were in a good shape financially, despite the bullshit with Trent, so it was completely doable.

"Alright, Remi, you got all the info inside?"

"Yup. You gonna go for it?"

"I think I am."

"I think it's a smart idea."

Before heading back into the shop, I snapped a picture of my soon-to-be food truck. I'd not seen Alec since his last visit a couple of weeks ago, but we'd still talked. With him doing most of the calling and checking in. I'd kept the fact I was exploring his idea to myself. The man had enough of an ego. I didn't need to go feeding it anymore. However, I couldn't stop the smile as I fired off a text to him.

Looks like I'm taking your suggestion.

No sooner than I hit send did the act stop me in my tracks. He'd officially became the first person I told. Sure, the others knew I was considering it, but... I shook it off. It didn't mean anything other than giving credit where credit was due.

The cool AC was welcomed once I entered the reception area. The weird scent of motor oil and Pine Sol mingled in the air in an odd but somewhat familiar way. The building may have been old, but Remi kept it organized and clean. She quickly plucked a manilla folder from the file rack on her desk.

"Here's everything you need. The owner's contact number, plus the card on where you can get the inside customized." She propped up, partially sitting on the worn metal surface.

"Thanks again. Seriously, I appreciate you going out of your way for this."

She waved me off. "Don't mention it. Look, it's the least I could do. If this place ever... It's not much, but it's mine, and I take pride in it. I suspect you're the same. We gotta look out for each other. Any word on how much longer?"

My nearly ever present low, painful throb ached in my temple. "Who the hell knows. Them insurance folks don't seem to be in any damn hurry. So much red tape. Pay premiums for years. Decades. And they want to drag their damn feet on the payout."

She pushed upright and huffed a laugh. "Damn. I hear ya. A real racket for sure." Remi rolled her shoulders. "You'll probably want to get it outfitted before I do the work, just for the weight and all."

I nodded, and my phone started buzzing. Seeing Alec's number brought a smile to my face.

"Imma get back to it and let you talk to whoever that is."

I glanced up to see her playful smirk coupled with a single arched brow. She disappeared behind the swinging glass door before I could even say anything. The offending contraption buzzed again. How did that man have me apparently grinning like a damn fool with a simple phone call?

I slid the green icon over and pushed it from my mind. "Hello."

"So, you're doing it? For reals?"

I exited the office and waved to Remi and the guys on my way to The Shack. "Seems that way. Remi found a truck, so gonna call the owner after I grab some lunch."

"Remi? Who is he?"

His question made my steps falter. "Um, Remi is the best damn mechanic I know short of *her* father. Anyway, it needs some work to get it bakery ready, but Momma and Tricia are on board so looks like I'll be the proud owner of a food truck."

"Wow. I honestly didn't think you'd do it."

As I entered the BBQ joint, the smell made my stomach growl. I stepped to the side and leaned against one of the back tables. "Why not?"

He laughed. "Mostly because I figured you'd reject it just to spite me."

"Why would you think that? I told you that day it was a good idea, just wasn't something I thought I could take on right now. And if I'm being honest, still not a hundred percent sure."

I massaged my neck, hoping in vain to lighten the weight that was trying to settle on me once again.

"I have all the faith in the world that you will pull this off in spectacular fashion. And I'm being serious. From the day we met you've had this drive, this passion to keep going and make the best of a bad situation. Failure doesn't seem to be an option for you."

His words managed to cause a tightening in my chest. Why his caring and investment in not only my business but in me affected me so damn much was a question I wasn't sure I wanted to answer. Regardless, it made me breathe just a little bit easier, which made no damn sense. Not since— Nope. I shook that off before the thought could even fully form. A weak time in my life, that's all this was.

❀ 18 ❀

ALEC

T HE BUZZING OF THE ALARM INTERRUPTED MY PEACEFUL slumber. Rolling over, I slapped at the off button before I swung my legs over the side of the bed and stretched. Between working my regular shifts and actually having more investigation work to do, this was my first real off day in weeks. Or was supposed to be until I'd gotten a call from Regina's insurance company.

Nearly a month later, they were finally sending out their own investigator and wanted me to walk through the bakery with them. But their findings were gonna be screwed because of the delay. I rolled my neck, wincing at the pops and cracks that followed. One upside to giving up my much looked forward to off day was getting to see Regina. I could not get that woman out of my system.

As I stepped into the shower, my mind went back to her being a widow. Maybe that played into it. But it was also a topic she didn't want to talk about. On top of me bringing up her dick-and-dash tendencies, it could make me come across as clingy. That was not who I was.

A phase. That's all this was. I had to get over myself and realize I had found me in female form with Regina Parker.

Whatever was happening with us would run its course, then we'd go our separate ways.

As crazy as it sounded, I was almost getting used to and enjoying the drive to Madison Island. It was picturesque in its charm. Mossy oak trees that seemed to be the unofficial mascot of the town. The square with its park benches, cobblestone paths, and lush grass. I could almost picture laying out on a blanket under one of those trees having a lazy picnic in the park with Regina.

I laughed and shook my head. If I didn't want to admit she was getting to me before, I sure as hell couldn't deny it if I was entertaining the fact that time in this town was something I actually looked forward to.

But the unmistakable pride everyone had in this place could not be denied.

It shone through in the upkeep of the place, the sense of community and support that was ever present. I'm sure it wasn't always smiles and unicorns, but on the surface, it sure as hell seemed that way.

I made my way down Main and easily found a parking spot in front of the bakery. The clock on my dash said it was only 10:30 so I'd expected the place to be busy due to Regina's pop-up shop, but it seemed no one was around other than a few people frequenting the other businesses. Worry kicked in. Was she alright? Had something else happened with that asshole who'd burned her place? She'd not said anything when I'd texted her to say I was coming. I grabbed my phone from the dash-mounted holder and fired off a text to her: *No bake sale today?* I smiled at the message. I was sure to get some sort of sassy reply for calling it a bake sale.

My phone buzzed. The side eye emoji was the first message. The second: *Nope, thought it best to be out of the way.*

She wasn't wrong. I was unclear on the legalities of her doing what she did in the parking lot, but I did know no one in this town would rat her out. I was, however, disappointed I wouldn't get to see her. At least not until after I was done with the insurance company.

A truck pulled up next to me, and I turned to see Chief Morris. I smiled at the older man and knew I'd be in for another one of his campaigns to get me to take over for him. He'd planted the seed the first time I'd been here, and brought it up again the morning I'd helped at Regina's pop-up shop. He wanted to retire. Again. And while he highly respected the men who volunteered their time at the station, the job was not their first priority. Which was understandable. It was supplemental income, though I had to think taking the only full-time city position offered in regard to the fire department had to be decent pay. It sure as hell would need to match if not beat what I was currently making.

"Alec, good morning to ya," he said, grasping my hand in a firm shake.

"Morning, Chief. How are you today?"

He adjusted the large flashlight hanging from his shoulder. "Old and tired. But can't complain."

I grinned and nodded. "Hopefully this won't take too long."

He ambled over to unlock the boarded-up door, and the little bell above it rang as he pushed it open. The day was bright and sunny, but with the lack of power and the plywood on the door and windows, the inside was dark and dank. The air was stale with lack of air circulation, and the charred odor mixed with possible mildew growth thanks to the heat and water. Nothing had been moved since I'd been inside last. Now knowing the woman behind the business, the destruction hit me differently. From the overturned chairs, bits of broken glass that crunched under my feet, and the menu sign that was half-erased with streaks of colorful chalk, all of it made my mouth go dry and my stomach drop. But it also surged a renewed anger through me that someone would hurt Regina in such a way. I made a mental note to stop by and see if the sheriff had any updates he'd be willing to share.

"Every time I drive by this place it hurts my soul," Chief commented with a heavy sigh.

Two knocks interrupted my reply. We turned to see an older, white, bald man in a dark-blue button-down and khaki cargo pants.

"Mornin', gentlemen. I'm Patrick Kincaid, sent out by Pillars Insurance."

I shook hands with the man who would either corroborate my findings or dispute them, which could screw Regina over if they denied her claim. After introductions were made, he popped a hard hat onto his head and flicked on the attached light.

We spent nearly two hours as he went over everything I'd put in my report page by page. He inquired about things, took pictures, threw in sly questions that I knew were meant to be an attempt to trip me up almost as if he somehow thought I'd faked my findings. Regardless of how annoyed I was at the whole ordeal, I kept my cool and professionalism. At the end of the day, the man worked for the insurance company, and arson was always tricky for payouts. By the time Patrick left, I had a good feeling he'd find in favor of Regina. And I couldn't wait to meet up with her to let her know how it went.

A smile stretched across my face as I leaned against my Jeep, waiting for Chief Morris to lock up.

He took the key off his ring as he walked toward me. "Get this back to her for me."

I wouldn't even try to deny I'd be seeing her, but the fact he already knew, or implied as much was one of those things that made me cringe about small towns. I put the key in my pocket and nodded.

He shoved his hands into his pockets and rocked back on his heels. "So, you give any more thought about the job?"

I rubbed my neck and laughed. "Still thinking, Chief. I have a lot to consider, mainly this role I'm currently in. And to be honest, I like the option of a bit more action than I think I'd see here."

He nodded slowly. "Can't do much about the action. But I suspect you working the investigation job means you wanted off the truck at some point."

He wasn't wrong, though I saw myself back in the city when that happened. And if I was being honest with myself, becoming a fire chief wasn't on my career plans. Too much administration work. More than I faced being the fire investigator, and that job still got me out in the field. In the time I'd been in Savannah, I couldn't recall the number of times Chief Johnson actually showed up on a scene. That life seemed like a slow death to me.

But Regina.

Yes, I wanted to spend more time with her. To get to know her better... Hell, my buddy Reggie might even call me pussy whipped, but was that enough for what would be a major life change?

I hit the unlock button on my Jeep. "I'll give it some more thought."

❦ 19 ❦

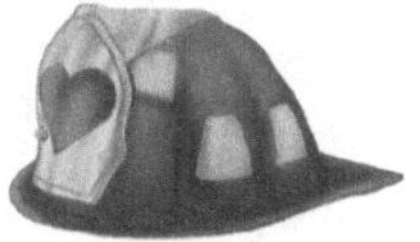

REGINA

I PULLED INTO A PARKING SPOT RIGHT NEXT TO ALEC'S EMPTY Jeep. I'd thought he would have simply headed to Blue Bird, but instead he'd asked me to meet him in town for lunch. The nerves in my stomach kept my appetite at bay. The insurance investigator stood between me and the payout I needed to start rebuilding. If all else failed, I was sure the community would come together to help get the business up and running again, but that burden shouldn't be on them.

I exited my SUV and glanced around, trying to find Alec to no avail. I pulled my phone from my bag and dialed his number.

He answered after the second ring. "Hello."

"You tell me to come down here, and you're not even around?"

I didn't want to acknowledge how comforting the sound of his laugh was.

"I'm across the street in the park, near the pond. Under one of these storybook oak trees."

My gaze drifted to the town center. The green space that was the hub of Madison Island. From concerts in the park, to town celebrations, to lazy days taking in the quiet peace, a lot went on at Founders Square. Living here for all my life, I'd gotten accustomed to everything, but to hear him call the large oaks found throughout the island storybook gave me pause.

I made my way across the street, scanning the areas close to the pond, trying to spot him. He wasn't hard to miss, leaning up against a tree looking like an image straight out of a magazine. The man was not afraid to wear pastels, and I had to admit they looked damn good against his dark complexion. The light-blue shirt he wore being no exception. Alec raised his hand and waved when he spotted me, and a large grin spread across his face, causing a warming feeling to shoot through me. Was I actually excited to see this damn man? I shook my head and said hellos to people on my way to him. Ignoring how my steps seemed to increase in pace. As soon as I was in reach, Alec pulled me into his arms and kissed me. It wasn't deep, just a fast, passionate hello, but it was enough to nearly make me forget we were out in public. I stepped back and pressed my lips together, finally noticing the blanket on the ground.

"What's all this?"

"Lunch. It's a nice day, and the park gives off a chill vibe. I thought a picnic would be good."

I arched a brow. "You planned a picnic?"

He lifted one shoulder. "Not planned per se, but the idea came to me as I was driving past. Chief Morris was kind enough to suggest Hubbard's deli as a great place to get sandwiches. Oh, and the owner said to tell you hello."

I blinked a few times. He'd set this up on the fly? Even going so far as to head to Hubbard's. And if they were saying hello, it had to mean Alec asked what I liked. As I lowered to the ground, I did my best to ignore the warming emotions attempting to take over. I was too old to be getting all giddy over some man. Even if said man was the epitome of sex on legs and showed his considerate side more times than I cared to admit.

"Are you buttering me up to deliver bad news?"

He eased down beside me with his brows drawn together. "Why do you always think I have ulterior motives?"

I picked up the brown bag, unfolding it to peer inside, and shrugged. It was easier to go that route first than to let myself acknowledge the meaningful date-like situation before me.

"So, if not bad news, is this you tryin' to court me?"

He laughed, the deep, rich sound that I was beginning to enjoy more than I should have. "Maybe I am, Ms. Parker." He reached into the bag and pulled out one of the sandwiches wrapped in white paper, then handed it to me after reading the label. "I opted for no cookies because none could compare to yours." His lopsided and dangerously sexy smile accompanied his statement.

I rolled my eyes. "You know I'm going to be the talk of the town now, right?" I asked, ignoring his comment. I glanced around, nodding at folks as they passed by with smiles on their faces.

He leaned back, resting one arm behind me as he moved closer. "I thought we already were after the fire station and then our date at the pizza spot. In fact..." Alec reached into his pocket and produced a key. "Chief said to get this back to you."

I reached out for the small piece of metal. "I was going to stop by the station to get it."

"Well, he must have known I was likely to see you first."

I ignored the implication. I didn't have time to think about what it meant or even if it should have meant anything. He'd said date. It wasn't a date then or now. It was just two...acquaintances sharing a meal. Nothing more. Nothing less.

I unwrapped my chicken salad sandwich and turned to face the pond instead of at my companion. A picnic in the park, something I hadn't done in years, not since Darnell was little. Something simple. Something easy. Without expectations. And something Alec had done for no reason. "Thank you for this."

"No thanks needed. I get to have a meal with the most interesting and beautiful woman in town."

I took a bite and chewed thoughtfully. "I suppose this will be your last trip, right? I can't see a reason that you'd have to come back now that the insurance agent has come by."

I risked a quick glance in his direction. A slight smile tugged at the corner of his lips as he chewed on his Reuben. He didn't answer me right away. Instead, he picked up his bottle of soda and took a long, slow drink from it. I swallowed the dryness in my mouth. I didn't know why it bothered me that he was torturing me with his silence. Or more so that I was annoyed—not really annoyed, but bothered—I could honestly say I was bothered by the fact that he might not come back. That this might be the last time I saw him.

Alec picked up a paper napkin and wiped his mouth. His half-grin stretched into a full one. "I don't know, Miss Parker. This town is starting to grow on me." He rolled his tongue along his bottom lip. "There are a few sights I haven't explored yet." He made zero attempt to mask his lustful, appreciative gaze in my direction. "Yeah, in fact I'm pretty damn sure I have plenty of reasons to keep coming back to Madison Island." He finished the statement with a large bite into his sandwich.

I rolled my eyes and shook my head, not acknowledging the giddy euphoria that tried to spread through me at his words. We were having fun. This was not going to be anything different than what I was used to. Regardless of what Cynthia and Irene and apparently the whole fucking town thought.

"Anyway, did the insurance adjuster have anything good to say? Hopefully something along the lines that they're cutting me a check next week?"

"I don't know about next week, but I have a good feeling they'll be cutting your check soon. Chief Morris sang your praises. Went on and on about how important this place was and definitely shut down any thoughts that you had anything to do with it. He even gave the investigator the sheriff's name and number cuz he brought up the situation surrounding Trent and the active investigation already pending against him. And that he was the main suspect for the fire."

My chest tightened just a little bit. While I tried not to dwell on it, the betrayal cut me too deep. Which made these moments of ease that more important. "I appreciate your help, Alec. I don't know if talking to the insurance companies and answering all those questions is typically in your job description, but I appreciate it."

"I didn't mind at all. How are things going with the food truck?"

"Good. Good. Got a great deal on the vehicle and the company that I hired to put it together said I should have it back as early as next week. And I'm actually kind of excited about it. I mean it's going to be a whole new thing to figure out, but at the end of the day it's good for the business, which is good for my family So, thank you for that as well."

Alec moved the items that sat between us and inched closer to me. He placed his hand on my back, the warmth from his palm seeped through the thin fabric of my shirt, and he pressed his lips to my shoulder. "I'm glad to hear it, Regina." He kissed my neck. "I have no doubt that it will be amazing." The low tenor of his voice, the scratch of his beard against my skin, and the fact his hand kept inching closer to my ass was a dangerous combination.

I pushed against his chest. "You can't be feeling me up in public."

He stole another quick kiss. "This is me behaving. Wouldn't want your father-in-law to arrest us for public indecency or something." He winked, but the mention of Pops had me glancing around the park.

It'd been sixteen years, and I was sure he didn't imagine I'd never date or anything again, but guilt lingered. Pops had spent the years working and being a doting grandfather to Darnell. He was by all accounts the devoted widower. Not that I wanted to think too hard—or at all—about my father-in-law's love life.

I cleared my throat and pushed the thought away. "Only one

of us will be arrested." I pinned him with a pointed look, and Alec laughed in response.

We finished our lunch in a comfortable silence. The seasons were changing. The leaves were starting to turn, and the oppressive heat was beginning to cool. Fall was upon us, and as I studied the area I'd been so many times before, I looked at it through new eyes. His eyes. I loved my town. The easy-going simplicity of it all. Sure, getting away for trips every now and again on vacation with my friends over the years was nice, but I always looked forward to coming home. To this quaint "storybook" place that held my highest highs and my lowest lows.

"You gonna tuck me in tonight?" Alec asked, pulling me from my thoughts. He'd cleaned up the trash and stood just off to the left with his hand held out to help me up.

"It's Friday. Cynthia has one set of guests tonight."

Alec wrapped his arms around my waist, pulling my body flush against his hard one. "Guess that means you can't be a screamer then."

I tilted my head up and narrowed my eyes at him. "Neither can you."

"Touché, Miss Parker. Touché."

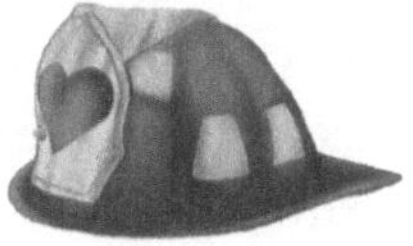

ALEC

I WOULDN'T BOTHER GETTING MY HOPES UP ON HAVING Regina stay the night with me. Sleepovers seemed to be her line in the sand, as was her house, and I would respect that. Even if I took a hit to my ego each time.

"You wanted to see some sights, right?" Regina asked as we crossed the street to our cars. "Not like that." She quickly added when a grin broke out on my face.

"Sure, what do you have in mind?"

She hit the fob on her chain. The lights flashed and the distinct sound of the locks opening clicked. "Hop in."

I tossed my newly purchased blanket into the back seat of her little SUV and climbed into the passenger side. The hours I'd just spent in her company hadn't been enough. It was strange. The more I was around her, the more I craved. Regina Parker was becoming an insatiable hunger. And it was more than the sex. It was her and everything she embodied. Her seriousness. Her playfulness. Even her sadness. The bit of turmoil that would show up in her eyes at the mention of her bakery or that Trent fucker. It wouldn't stay for long. But it would spark just a bit before the strong and capable side took over once more.

I noticed we'd driven out of the center of town and were heading out of the city. "Where are we going?"

"To a hidden gem," she replied. A soft smile on her face as she glanced at me briefly.

"Am I about to become the Wicker Man?"

She let out a cackle and nodded. "Maybe, Special Investigator. Maybe."

As we approached the covered bridge that was the signal you were about to enter into a whole new world, Regina shocked me by going off-road. I'd driven this route plenty of times as of late and I'd never noticed the narrow path. The terrain was rough, and I was doubting her vehicle's off roading worthiness.

I placed one hand on the roof and the other on the dash. "You know, maybe we should have taken my Jeep instead."

Regina swayed with the bumps and dips as she kept driving down the dirt road that seemed to narrow instead of widening. "Eh, it's all good."

No sooner did she say that, we broke through the trees and bushes to a clearing.

She screeched to a halt then killed the engine. "See? We arrived in one piece."

I stared out the window while she climbed free of the car. It was a swamp...maybe. It had the same sort of look as the marsh behind the bed and breakfast. This was the hidden gem?

I shook my head as I exited and followed Regina toward one of the largest trees I'd ever seen. It was like the mossy oaks that seemed to be the main make-up of the scenery of Madison Island, but different. Its branches draped in dramatic fashion, with some dipping to disappear in the murky water.

The trunk didn't seem to be one solid piece, but instead was an intricate woven combination of many. There was an odd beauty to it. Behind the canopy of delicate branches was a large collection of boulders, which was where Regina had sat. She leaned back on her hands, her eyes closed and the most content expression on her face. I almost didn't want to disrupt the peace that seemed to come over her almost instantly.

I crept closer as quietly as I could and took a seat beside her. I took the opportunity to truly drink in her appearance as the sounds of nature made its music. It was almost as if this was the first time I was seeing her. The real her. Her outspoken personality was her, but she was a woman of many layers. Losing her business like she had, there was pain there that she didn't want people to see, but as we sat on the large rock, the weight she carried seemed to lift, if only for a brief moment.

"There's only been one time in my life I ever thought about leaving Madison." Regina sat up and glanced at me briefly before looking out over the water. "I'd gotten in my car and headed out of town but spontaneously turned my wheel and ended up on this random dirt road. Something brought me here. I'd lived in Madison my whole life and never knew this place existed until that day."

She paused and took a few breaths. On some out of body instinct, I wrapped my hand around hers as she quietly wrestled with whatever memory. Which I suspected had to do with when she'd lost her husband.

"Anyway, I got out of my car and just screamed until I couldn't anymore. It was very cathartic. Afterward, I sat on this boulder and contemplated life. Then got in my car and drove home. It's become my place when I need to be lost for a little while. And it reminds me of why I stay and what all I've built."

She rested her head on my shoulder and I took in the previously unimpressive surroundings with new appreciation. Regina had let me in. She'd brought me to a place that was personal and had deep meaning to her. I ran my thumb across her knuckles as an expansive warmth spread through my chest. She'd opened up, shared a piece of herself...that coming from a woman who hid behind flirting, sass, and sex... The significance of the moment made me sit a little straighter as I curled my fingers around hers.

She'd let me in.

WHEN I WALKED into the B&B, Cynthia greeted me in the foyer. "Alec. How are you this evening?"

"Good. And thank you for squeezing me in tonight."

"No worries. My guests for tomorrow won't be here until three, so plenty of time to change it over." She strolled over to the wall cabinet Regina had pulled the key from last time, unlocked it, and handed me a set. "Here you go. You'll be in the same room as last time." The knowing look on her face made me chuckle to myself.

She turned and headed up the stairs. "Come on, I'll show you up, even though you should know the way." We stopped outside the Hummingbird suite. "I wanted to ask you, I got a reservation by the name of Delores and William Hodge. Any relation?"

"Yes, ma'am. Those would be my parents. I told them about your place and the town. I'm happy they booked a stay."

I hadn't talked to them much since Mia's birthday party. A series of missed calls and basic texts had been our communication for the past few weeks. I made a mental note to check in with them. Their visit would give me another reason to come back to Madison sooner rather than later. I couldn't have my parents so close and not see them. What kind of son would that make me?

"Well, thank you for the advertisement. I can use all the help I can get."

"From what Regina says, you're already doing well only being opened for a few months."

Echoes from the stairs made us turn in time to see Marcel making his way up. When he laid eyes on his wife, his body language seemed to change. He stood a little straighter and grinned wide. It was subtle, but it was there. I glanced at Cynthia, who kept her attention on the man approaching, holding her hand out toward him. When their fingers touched, the spark of their connection buzzed in the air, and I felt like I was intruding on some sort of private, intimate moment.

He leaned to give her a quick kiss before greeting me. "Alec, good to see you."

"Same." I adjusted my bag to shake his hand.

"Baby, I'm gonna go hop in the shower." Marcel kissed his wife again, said his goodbye to me, and disappeared behind the door at the end of the hall.

"I'll let you get settled. Regina should be here shortly. You'll join us for dinner, won't you?" Cynthia asked.

"Um, you sure it's not an imposition?"

"Not at all. I'll text Regina so she knows to stop by your room to get you before she comes up."

Alone in my room, I hopped into the shower for a quick freshen up. Dinner with Regina and her friends, almost like a double date. I laughed as soon as the thought popped into my mind. By the time the knock sounded at my door, I'd redressed in a simple black V-neck and light gray joggers. She also had changed, and when I laid eyes on the denim dress, I ran my tongue along the front of my teeth and nodded slightly.

The corners of her mouth tugged upwards, an indication she knew what I was thinking about her outfit. "Ready?"

I turned to grab the key from the dresser and stepped out. "I haven't been on a double date since high school. This should be fun."

She shot me a side eye. "There you go with that date business again."

"I'm courtin' you, remember?"

She paused with her hand on the knob. "Is that so?"

I looked her directly in her light brown eyes and realized in that moment, all joking aside, I was in fact trying to date Regina Parker. The words my mother had spoken hit me like a freight train. The day spent with Regina had been different and I couldn't put a finger on why until now. It had been more than her opening up to me at the clearing. It'd been the whole vibe of the day from dealing with the insurance guy, to having the picnic in the park. A protective, I need to take care of her, side of me had been fully activated. It was something I didn't think I was capable of or even knew existed until her. She was the woman who had changed my whole world, and she had no fucking clue.

"Yes." I reached around her to open the door then bent at the waist with flourish. "After you, madam."

21

REGINA

I BLINKED ONCE, THEN TWICE BEFORE TURNING AND CLIMBING up the stairs to Cynthia's owner's suite and did my best to ignore whatever just happened less than thirty seconds ago. Maybe him being done with the investigation and staying in Savannah was for the best.

I'd been kicking myself since we'd left the clearing. Why had I taken him there? And why had I opened up to him? I'd never told anyone I'd thought about leaving Madison after Lawrence had died.

"Perfect timing," Cynthia stated when I crested the top of the steps. She was setting a serving dish on the island.

Soft jazz played from the Bluetooth speaker, and the inviting space smelled of a wonderful mix of chicken, herbs, and all-around deliciousness.

"Beer or wine?" Marcel asked, directing the question to Alec as Cynthia was already pouring a glass of red for me.

"Beer's good. And thank you again for inviting me."

"The more the merrier," Cynthia replied. "Plus, it'll be good to get to know you better."

I shot her a look, which she shrugged off behind a smug grin.

Over dinner, Cynthia and Marcel—mostly Cynthia—quizzed Alec about everything from family to his job. Like the conversations we had, he answered easily and honestly. He and Marcel even bonded over talk of sports, with them both being big fans of the Falcons despite their record and Alec getting into the Atlanta United team. My interest in sports was nil so Cynthia and I finished off a bottle of wine watching them go back and forth over trades, how they hoped the season would go, and playoff dreams. It was odd, yet eerily comforting, how easily he seemed to fit in with my closest friends.

"Oh, Regina, I want to show you a few things," Marcel said as we cleared the table. "MJ has been getting fancy and has some ideas if you were open to a few redesigns once we start the reconstruction."

He ducked into the room and came back with his laptop. Marcel set it up on the island, and I tried to ignore how close Alec sat to me so he could peek at the screen. I wouldn't turn my head to take in a deeper inhale of his clean, spicy aroma with a hint of citrus. A smelled that reminded me of a warm fire on a cold winter night and I wanted to get as close as possible. I was a moth to his flame. I shuttered at the thought, and he absent-mindedly ran his hand up and down my arm while Marcel explained the designs.

MJ had worked up two different options. The first being similar to what we'd had, but the second would turn the dining area into more of a lounge. Less tables and more booths or couches inviting people to sit, converse, and stay a while.

"These are amazing," Alec commented leaning closer to the screen. "I don't think I've ever seen anything quite like this." He turned to me, giving my leg a light squeeze just above my knee. "That's what we're trying to get you back to? I would drive forty plus minutes out of my way to get coffee here."

The wine. It had to be the wine that made me lightheaded and constricted my breathing for a moment. Not the sound of wonder, and certainly not the clear support and awe found in

Alec's words. The "we" sent my heart racing and raised goose-bumps on my arms.

I glanced up and locked eyes with my friend, who gave me a gentle smile in return. What the fuck was happening?

"That's the hope," Marcel replied. "We are ready and willing the moment we get the green light."

Alec glanced around. "You did all of this?"

"My man is talented," Cynthia answered, sliding her arm around Marcel's waist. "He's the best contractor on the island."

"I'm the only contractor on the island."

She stretched up to give him a kiss. "Still the best. Our guests have nothing but great things to say, and that's all thanks to you."

I'd been around Cynthia and Marcel plenty. Their clear love and devotion to each other was nothing new. But after today, being around Alec, hearing his declaration to "courting" me, for the first time in a long time I missed having that someone special. I missed having someone to lean on. Yes, I had Cynthia and Irene. I had my momma and daddy, but they were all differ-ent. It wasn't quite the same as having someone to come home to. It wasn't the same as having someone to talk to at the end of a trying day. And it wasn't something I'd had time for.

But in the face of it, it was painfully obvious I was missing that level of intimacy.

"I like your friends," Alec commented as we headed back to his room. "They're good people. And I can't believe that you all have known each other since elementary school. I mean, I talk to one or two of my friends from high school, but nothing like what you have. We keep in touch mainly through a couple of fantasy sports leagues. I'm pretty astonished how y'all have maintained."

We stopped in front of his door. "I guess I never really thought about it. We each put in the effort even after Cynthia moved away, and with Irene still gone. We each made the choice to make us and our friendship a priority."

I'd never pictured our thirty-plus-year-long friendship as

anything out of the norm. We simply were. Through thick and thin, we persisted. And it wasn't to say we never had disagreements and that everything was always sunshine and rainbows. That would be unrealistic. Respect came in many forms, as did love. And I loved those women and always would. Over the years, we'd proved multiple times that the feeling was mutual.

Alec unlocked his door. "You gonna tuck me in?"

I reached up to stroke his face, letting my thumb glide back and forth across his surprisingly smooth skin. When I stretched up on my tiptoes, he bent, allowing our lips to connect in a sweet, but brief kiss.

"Going to have to take a rain check, Special Investigator. I need to get home and do some prep work. I'll see you in the morning cuz I have to bring by pastries for Cynthia's guests."

His disappointment was evident as he leaned against the doorframe and let out a low sigh. "No bake sale in the morning?"

I shook my head. "No. I'm a pretty capable woman, but this whole thing is definitely more work, and because of my obligations here, trying to do both on the weekends just isn't feasible. That might change when I get my truck. Who knows."

He stepped forward, and I was once again pulled into his arms. "You are more than capable, Regina Parker. And you can do damn near anything you set your mind to. Of that I have no doubt."

Alec leaned and kissed me again. This time letting his disappointment in not getting laid come through. His tongue teased my bottom lip in a silent request for entry, which I happily obliged. I gripped at his arms. He grabbed handfuls of my ass, and I couldn't stop the little moan from escaping the back of my throat.

Damn, this man could kiss. His expert exploration made my head swarm and my stomach do flops. His growing stiffness between us was a clear sign I wasn't the only one with a rising arousal.

I pulled back, needing the air that recirculated in my lungs to help clear my head from all the confusing thoughts. "Is that your attempt at trying to get me to stay?"

His signature panty melting smirk appeared. "Maybe."

I shook my head and laughed. "I always make good on my rain checks, don't I?"

"That you do, Miss Parker. That you do."

I patted his chest lightly three times quickly before untangling myself from his embrace. "See you in the morning, Special Investigator."

"Goodnight, Regina."

As I drove home, I thought about what Alec had said about being able to do anything I set my mind to. If only that were true. Because I couldn't seem to stop myself from catching feelings for Special Investigator Alec Hodge.

❧ 22 ❧

ALEC

"HODGE, IN MY OFFICE AFTER YOU STORE YOUR GEAR," CHIEF Johnson bellowed from his doorway.

I dropped my head back and stared at the concrete ceiling of the bay for half a beat.

Sasha laughed as she pushed by me. "No rest for the wicked."

All I wanted after that last call was a shower and to chill out on my cot. Instead, I lugged my stuff over to the lockers with the rest of the gang. I quickly stored it away knowing I'd have to go back and clean it and check my tanks before I got the much desired but sadly lukewarm shower after seeing what the boss wanted.

Even though I'd been summoned, I still knocked on the frame and waited for him to wave me in before I entered. He thrust a sheet of paper toward me before I had a chance to sit.

"Your investigator duties call."

For half a second, my heart seized in fear that somehow Regina would be involved again. She hadn't given any updates on the investigation in regard to if Trent was back in custody or not. I blinked and focused on the form I'd been handed. Richmond Hill. Not Madison Island. In the opposite direction in fact.

The momentary tension uncoiled. "When do they want me?"

"I told him you're on duty today, so they said they're fine with you coming tomorrow. I already called in Joe to take the other half of your shift."

Joe was the newest guy on the team, which meant he got the worst schedule. He was the last to pick, and he was also on call whenever I had to head out and handle an investigation. He was a young guy, eager and straight out of high school. He reminded me of myself in some ways.

"All right is there anything else, sir?"

Chief leaned back in his chair, groaning in dramatic fashion while linking his hands behind his head. "The fire chief from your first assignment reached out to me."

New panic. I knew Chief Morris was eager to have me take over for him. The man was ready to fully retire and spend more time with his grandchildren down in Florida. But I still wasn't sure small-town living was the life I wanted. Since my first trip and we'd made small talk about my possible career plans, he'd planted the idea of me having my own station at some point. Mainly the one in Madison, though he'd tried to camouflage it as a general move to chief and not the cherry picked position he wanted me to take. He wasn't hounding me or anything, but he had not been shy about making his wishes known whenever we'd seen each other. I had to hope him reaching out to my chief wasn't an attempt to shoehorn me into taking the position I wasn't sure I wanted. A thought hit me. I was all gung-ho to try and date Regina, but I hadn't stopped to fully let what that meant sink in until that moment. Her roots were deep in Madison Island. A business, family, close friends. If something between us went anywhere, it would be me, not her making the sacrifice to move.

But I was getting ahead of myself. Way fucking ahead.

I slid into the creaky chair opposite the desk. "What did he need?"

Chief Johnson shifted forward, tented his hands, and rested his chin on them. "He wants you to do a training. He said something about how that fire you investigated, while they handled it and kept it under control without having to call an extra department, made him realize his guys could use some more training. Some updated skills and techniques since he's been out of the business for years and is more a 'figurehead,' in his words. You seem to have made quite the impression upon him."

I suppressed the laugh threatening to escape. "I don't know about that, sir. The entire department consists of about eight guys that work on a rotating, volunteer basis. That's it. They know the basics. Just enough to get the job done."

Chief nodded. "That's par for the course for those volunteer departments. If you want to do it, you can try and work something out. He did say that the town would pay you for your time. But it would definitely ease the added burden if you could try and schedule it for your off days, so we won't be short-handed any more than required for your investigative duties."

"Yes, sir, understood."

"Clean up and get some rest." His dismissal was clear.

After getting my gear properly taken care of and grabbing a much-needed shower, I dialed up Chief Morris to talk to him about what he wanted me to do. He let me know he only wanted me to run through some basic drills and possibly show some new techniques. Nothing too major. What they handled outside of Regina's big fire was usually all small-scale stuff. However, it was always good to have a refresher just in case. We would wait a few weeks so that he could give the guys time to coordinate their off days with their day jobs since he wanted them all to be in attendance.

I had never officially been in charge of training anyone before, but this new opportunity was exciting. My career couldn't be stagnant. And this would give me an addition to my resume. Being a jack of trades was useful in the long run. At my old department, and even at my current one, we regularly did trainings and simulations to keep our skills up. In most cases, there was usually a trainer involved, and at both locations the chiefs were there to help give instruction, if not participate. I knew Chief Morris was up to something, and his request was probably just another ploy in his recruitment arsenal, but I'd take any and every opportunity I had to get back to Regina.

❦

I HATED that I missed the "grand opening" of her food truck, but I'd called to congratulate her and sent flowers. In the weeks leading up to the big day, Regina had kept me in the loop on the progress. It'd been great that she'd shared with me and let me be part of it even if I'd not known all the ins and outs. I'd fed off her energy and was excited she was excited.

Plus, I'd followed opening day via her bakery's Instagram page. The business was the only social media she appeared to have, and I couldn't blame her. I didn't have an account until I created one with the express purpose of seeing how things were going. I told myself it wasn't creepy since she had given me her card, which had all the information listed on it. The image she'd texted me of her, her mother, and her niece smiling as they all cut a ribbon was seared into my brain. I took a little bit of the credit for that moment, having planted the idea. But making it come to fruition was all on the shoulders of the woman I was eager to see.

Hammering, buzzing, and yelling rang out in my ears as I exited my Jeep. The other thing I'd seen on her page? Reconstruction was underway. Some insurance companies could take forever, dragging their feet, especially in an arson case. It'd been nearly three months since the fire, but I was happy to see once the claim had been approved, her company had done right by her. First thing I noticed was that the previously broken windows had been replaced. Clear panes stood where the old ones once were. I peeked into the open door and saw the entire inside completely gutted. The swinging door which had separated the front and back was now just a gaping hole in the wall.

Even the chalkboard menu was gone. I'd only seen it in the destroyed state, but the emptiness of the space was jarring to me. How was Regina handling it?

"Hey, Alec." Marcel waved as he strolled toward me. He removed his hard hat and wiped a rag over his head. "Whatcha think?"

"It's, um, a lot to take in."

"Yeah. Yeah. But we have to tear it out before we can rebuild. Give me about nine weeks or so and it'll be like the fire never happened."

"I can't wait to see it in all its glory."

"Hey, Dad," a young guy called out from the entry way that led to the back.

"Welp, duty calls. But glad to see you. We'll have to do dinner again sometime." He raised a hand as he walked off.

Another invite. This town and its residents were starting to grow on me. One in particular for sure. I headed around back and spotted the object of my desire standing inside the little blue truck talking with her mother.

"Well, well, look what the cat dragged in," Mrs. Charles said with a large smile. "Good to see you again."

"You too, ma'am."

She waved her hand like she was swatting away a fly. "Pish with all that ma'am nonsense. You call me Mable or Mama Charles. Don't need nothin' else to make these old bones feel older."

"Oh, so now you old?" Regina chimed in.

Mable once again swatted the air. "Hush, child. Alec, be a dear and come on round the back and help me out this tiny ass box she got me slavin' in."

I moved to the rear of the truck just as she opened the door. A small set of stairs automatically unfolded, and I held my hand out to help her down.

She linked her arm through mine. "You'll help an old woman to her car, won'tcha?"

I glanced over my shoulder to see Regina propped up in the doorway.

"Imma tell Daddy you out here gettin' fresh."

"Snitches get stitches," Mrs. Charles yelled back.

I pressed my lips together to keep from laughing at the exchange. She fished keys out of her apron pocket, and I couldn't mask my surprise when the lights flashed on the sleek, black Ford Mustang.

"Don't look so shocked. I'm retired. Not dead. I can handle this and a whole lot more." She eased her large frame into the driver's seat and looked back toward her daughter. "And so can she. It was nice seein' ya again. Oh, and have her bring you 'round tonight for a fish fry."

I stepped back as she reached to close the door then revved the engine a few times before pulling off.

I strolled back to the truck shaking my head. "Your mom is something else."

"That's putting it mildly."

"And you've been instructed to bring me to dinner tonight."

She planted her fists on her hips. "Say what now?"

I shrugged. "I can't go against your momma. She said she's having a fish fry and you're to bring me." I didn't attempt to stop the grin from forming in response to the scowl on Regina's face.

Laying eyes on her again after weeks of not seeing her brought me a level of peace I'd never experienced. I'd been stressed and unsettled. Restless whether at work or home. We'd talked, and hearing her voice had helped, but it was a mere Band-Aid.

The change I'd witnessed in Marcel that day at the B&B made so much sense as I stood in front of Regina. The sight of her alone released tension and lifted my mood. Even with the frowns, eye rolls, and feisty attitude directed at me more times than not.

And I hated that the two days I had in Madison would leave me very little time with her. The training would be at least twelve hours each day to get in everything I'd come up with based on my own drills and talking it over with my chief. It was solid, and the volunteers would be better for it, but still, damn the time it would consume.

With that thought in mind, I climbed into the truck and pulled Regina into my arms. An audible sigh poured from my lips the moment we came in contact.

She craned her neck up to look at me. "You okay there?"

"I am now."

❦ 23 ❦

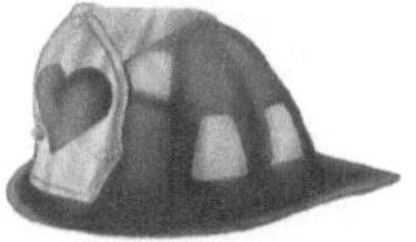

REGINA

THE WAY HE LOOKED AT ME STOLE MY BREATH. HIS DARK EYES held longing. But more than that, they held comfort and hope. Those were the eyes of a man who'd found his home, and that scared the shit out of me.

My brain didn't have time to acknowledge the warning signs. His hands were on my cheeks and his lips covering mine. Slow and unrushed. Alec kissed me with a tenderness and appreciativeness I'd not experienced since... I ran my hands up his back, clawing at the fabric and sinking into the moment. My heart squeezed as I moaned against him, letting go of my fears and restrictions on getting involved past anything physical. I simply allowed the what-ifs, the possibility of more to takeover.

"I've missed you," he whispered against my mouth before stepping back.

Though in the small confines of my truck, there wasn't much space to be had between us. Not that it mattered. His presence seemed to fill every nook and cranny.

"I couldn't tell. Back to collect on that rain check?" I needed to rebuild those barriers. To get us back on a course that was comfortable and safe.

"I consider that a perk, but not the reason I'm here."

"Ah, right, the training."

"Yeah, and you. Just you."

I turned away before I got sucked back into that earlier feeling. "What do you think?" I asked, changing the subject. I was proud of how the food truck turned out, and a part of me wanted Alec's stamp of approval, or something of that nature.

He took in the space, nodding with a smile on his face. "I like it. I've never been on the inside of one of these, but damn, you have it decked out."

His praise warmed me from the crown of my head down to my toes. Damn him.

"Thank you. I was surprised with all they could fit in here, but man, it's made a huge difference. Still not doing the same numbers, but doing better than I was."

"I had no doubt." He leaned against the stainless-steel counter and crossed his arms. "I peeked inside the building. Glad to see everything underway. That has to make you happy."

"Yes. Marcel said about two months or so, maybe sooner depending on how many men he can have on it and how behind the building inspectors are. But I'm ready."

"I won't miss that grand reopening. Come hell or high water, I'll be here for your big day."

Another zing of warmth buzzed through me. I started closing down, needing my focus to be on something, anything but the man taking up too much space. I was still fighting to get back on balance after the kiss and everything it meant. I couldn't fend off another attack of my barriers when my defenses were still weakened.

Without a word, Alec began helping me lock the front window and store the cleaned and dried utensils so they'd be ready for the next day. Then, much like he'd helped my momma, he held his hand out as I stepped down the small stairs.

"I've been thinking," he said from behind me as I locked the door.

"About?"

"I need to take you on a proper date."

I spun to face him. "There you go again."

"I don't know why you keep acting surprised. I've already told you my intentions."

I walked to the front of the truck with him trailing right beside me. "Right, because you have it in your mind to date me."

"Yup. And I need to take you out. Come to Savannah."

"What?"

"Next week I have Saturday and Sunday off. Drive to Savannah, and let me take you on a proper outing. We probably won't be able to see each other for the holidays, but we can do something beforehand."

He was too much, and I was having emotional sensory overload. And even though the logical part of my brain, the part that had kept me protected from all things relationship-related said to abort mission, the no that should have been on the tip of my tongue somehow wasn't. Special Investigator Alec Hodge had somehow managed to get past my defenses. "Fine."

The troublemaking, panty-melting grin made an appearance. "Did you just agree? That easily?"

I planted my hands on my hips. "Don't get all cocky and make me change my mind."

He pulled me into his arms. There weren't many people around, but enough that I was aware, but also didn't care as much as I should when he placed a chaste kiss on my lips. "Too late. What time is dinner?"

I groaned. Right, dinner at my parents'. Just what I needed. "I have to go home and shower. You stayin' at the station this time, right?"

"Unfortunately. Unless you're offering me room and board."

I pushed free of his embrace. "Man, please. But I'll swing by and pick you up around four."

I CONTINUALLY ASKED myself what the hell I was doing as I made my way through town to go retrieve my forced upon me dinner date. Momma was always meddling. I wasn't sure what annoyed me more. Her invite, or the fact he'd agreed to a meal with my parents without a second thought. For some reason, the universe and everyone around me was in cahoots against me when it came to Special Investigator Alec Hodge.

His black Jeep gleamed in the sun, making me wonder how much time he spent cleaning it. The interior had also been spotless. No trash, extra clothes, or general clutter. His car was as immaculate as he always presented. It'd even smelled good, just like him. I put my SUV in park next to his vehicle. He couldn't simply be outside waiting for me, could he? No, I'd have to go in and add to the town gossip.

No one was in the bay area when I walked through the large garage doors. I'd never had much need to visit the firehouse before, so I was unsure of where to go, but I followed the sound of voices toward the interior of the building. After making my way through the glass doors at the far end of the station, I found a small living room type of area. There I located the guys, including the one I was after, sitting around on drab furniture yelling at a large flat screen TV.

Perched on the arm of a chair, Alec easily chatted with one of the others. I couldn't help but wonder if there was anyone he didn't get along with. Cynthia and Marcel had welcomed him into the fold. Irene hadn't even met him in person, but she too seemed to be Team Alec just from our conversations. And hell, I was here, to pick him up for dinner because he'd certainly won over my momma.

He turned and the moment he laid eyes on me a lazy grin spread across his face. "There's my beautiful date."

The others looked, and greetings ensued before the next big play stole their attention again. Mostly. As he approached me, I was fully aware of the guys interested glances at the soft kiss he placed on my cheek and how he intertwined his fingers with mine.

"What no flowers? Ms. Parker you have to work on your wooing skills," he joked.

I rolled my eyes. "I'm not trying to woo you, Special Investigator. And this isn't a date. You are my momma's guest, not mine."

The guys laughed at my comeback. Meanwhile, Alec was completely unbothered as he lifted our joined hands to his mouth and kissed mine. "You say the most romantic things." He said his goodbyes to the fellas and led us out of the station.

He didn't release his hold on me until he stopped at his vehicle. "I wasn't sure if your dad drank or not, so I have soda and beer." He pulled a bag from a cooler in the back. "And, for you." He turned, producing a bouquet." The colorful mix of flowers included orange roses, sunflowers, lilies, and lavender. "Luckily for you, my wooing skills are top notch."

I took the offered package and brought it to my nose. It smelled divine, and I didn't want to acknowledge how receiving flowers was my happy place. "Thank you. It's a beautiful arrangement."

He shut the door of his Jeep and hit the key fob to lock it again. "Not as beautiful as you." He planted a quick kiss on my lips then placed his hand on my back to guide me to my car.

The drive to my parents' house seemed to take longer than ever. I blamed the slowing of time on the man beside me with his long legs and his hypnotic scent filling up the space in my small SUV. That, and all the genuine questions he asked about the construction of the bakery. I was shocked when asked if it would look the same as before since he'd not seen it. The sheepish look he got when admitting to following the social media sites Tricia set up made me laugh, but it also touched at that corner of my heart he kept tapping into no matter how much I attempted to keep him out.

I turned onto the paved road that started my parents' property.

"This is a lot of land," Alec commented.

"Yeah, I suppose it is. It's eight acres my dad and his brother inherited from their parents." I pointed to the first house on the left. "My grandparents used to live there. Now one of my cousins and his wife have moved in. The blue and white cottage is my uncle and aunt. She'd wanted to live closer to the beach, not the marsh, so he built her a beach house as a compromise."

We continued down the long road until we got to my parents' sprawling ranch-style home. It'd grown in size over the years as they expanded and added on to it. Much like Cynthia's place, the property backed up to the marsh. Dad had a nice deck built and spent plenty of time out there since retirement. The detached garage housed his boats and pickup.

"Wow, so y'all basically have a subdivision."

I parked in the circular drive. "Guess you could say that. Tricia has plans to build after graduation. I'd considered it at one time, but we ended up living in town instead. It worked out. As much as I love my family, I didn't need all the extra togetherness of being neighbors. Oh. And I guess I should tell you now, if you haven't already guessed, dinner will be pretty much all of them, not just my parents."

I probably took too much pleasure in the momentary look of terror that filtered across his face. He'd been throwing me off for far too long, it was nice to turn the tables on him.

❊ 24 ❊

ALEC

I THOUGHT MY FAMILY GET TOGETHERS WERE LEGENDARY, BUT the simple dinner I'd been expecting to attend was putting every party my parents had ever thrown to shame. They had a golf cart parking pad for the family members who lived on the property, complete with a special sign.

From the front, the home appeared to be a basic ranch with an expansive front porch. Homey and inviting. But around back was where the action happened. It was like being transported to another element. The outdoor kitchen setup was enviable, with both a gas and charcoal grill. They didn't just have a mini fridge for drinks, Mr. Albert Charles had a tap from which he poured his home brew. I couldn't imagine anything more impressive in the city. They even had an outdoor fireplace, which was roaring to fend off the cool night air, and a large TV under a pergola that was tied into a sound system which currently poured out old school disco. I guess when you lived on eight acres with only family as neighbors, breaking a noise ordinance was not an issue. That and the fact the sheriff was in attendance, along with Chief Morris. Not to mention the fish fry included crawfish and crab.

This was how small-town folks got on?

And Regina was totally in her element. During the time I'd

spent in Madison and around her and those I'd come in contact with, I understood the community aspect. I'd understood how the town had rallied and the connections she had with her employees and friends and, of course, her mother. Mrs. Charles was a force—just like her daughter.

I didn't know where this would go with us. Yes, I'd been pursuing her and wanted to attempt exclusive dating again for the first time in years, but being a part of the night's events reinforced the notion a sacrifice on one of our parts would be in order. My sacrifice.

"Food's ready," Mrs. Charles hollered.

I stood back and witnessed how they all fell into line like an assembly, loading up their trays. Notably absent was my date for the evening.

"Alec, you ain't hungry?" Mrs. Charles yelled, which made all eyes turn my way.

"I'm just waiting, ma'am."

She moved from behind the buffet table, mumbling under her breath. The sound of laughter made me turn to my left.

"You're in trouble now, Special Investigator."

Just as Regina said the words, her mother stood before me, hands on her hips and a frown on her face. "Boy, if you don't get your narrow ass in there and get something to eat... Gina, load him up good."

"He can fix his own plate."

"Don't sass me, girl. Do right and fix your man a plate."

Some of the family around snickered at the exchange. Regina moved around me and grabbed one of the Styrofoam platters. "You invited him, so technically, he's your guest," she grumbled.

Her mother pulled the towel from her shoulder and flicked it to hit Regina's butt.

I picked up a container of my own and leaned down to whisper to Regina. "Looks like you're the one in trouble."

"You get on my nerves."

I laughed. "Hopefully, later, I can get on something else."

She glared at me before breaking out into a large grin. Dinner acquired, we settled at the end of the table next to her cousins. I loved seafood, and knowing this was as fresh as it got had me savoring each bite. Sitting so close to Regina while she sucked the heads of the crawfish sent my thoughts racing down the gutter probably faster than it should have. I had no doubt if I ever got the pleasure of those lips on my dick, she'd damn near suck the soul from my body. I shifted in my seat and attempted to force the inappropriate fantasies away. At least for when we weren't in mixed company.

All random chit chat stopped as Mr. Charles approached our end of the table with a mason jar half-filled with a clear liquid.

He held it out to me. "Here, try this." His gruff tone made it seem more like an order rather than a simple offering. Or at least I hoped it wasn't an order.

"Daddy."

"What? It's just a little 'shine. Wanna know what the man thinks."

Regina leaned forward to look down the table. "Momma, come get your husband."

Mrs. Charles cracked open a crab leg and bit into the meat before shouting. "What for?"

A sniff of the liquid burned my nostrils, with the imaginary smoke clogging my throat and making me cough. Holy shit, what was in this battery acid? The laughs from those around me didn't make me feel any better. I was clearly being tested and had apparently failed part one.

"Don't look so skeptical. Sheriff is here. Not like I'm tryin' to kill ya or something. Just puttin' a little hair on ya chest."

I glanced at Regina, whose eyes were wide, and her normally full lips were pressed together in a hard line. It'd been a long-ass time since I'd felt like I was being dared to do something, yet I found myself in that exact situation. Time to man up. I took a healthy sip. Damn near instantly, my eyes watered, my tongue seemed to double in size, and I was pretty fucking sure I had chemical burns down my esophagus. I covered my mouth and did my damnedest to not sputter liquid as I tried to cough and swallow at the same time.

I was pretty fucking sure I looked like one of those cartoon characters with smoke billowing out of their ears. I was vaguely aware of Regina patting my back and handing me a glass, but I shook my head.

"It's just water," she spoke between laughs. "Damn it, Daddy, which one did you give him?"

Her father sputtered out a husky chuckle. "My extra special blend. That's the Mabel."

My vision refocused in time to see him wink toward his wife.

"How was it?" he inquired with a wicked grin on his face.

I took another sip of water and pounded my fist to my chest a couple of times. "Good." The high-pitched squeak of my voice brought on more laughs.

He patted my shoulder. "I had to make sure you could handle her."

"The moonshine, sir?"

He sucked his teeth and shook his head. "Nah. My baby girl. And I think you might be alright. Don't let good 'shine go to waste. Finish that on up." He jutted his chin toward the jar of certain death should I consume more, then ambled off.

Show over, everyone returned to eating like I hadn't had my life flash before my eyes moments ago. I had no idea how surviving that strong, homegrown liquor was a testament to me and my relationship with his daughter, but he appeared satisfied. I guess it was better than being threatened with an ass whooping or other such father protecting their daughter anecdotes.

"You okay?" Regina asked. Her warm brown eyes searched my face as she cupped my cheek.

I nodded. "Yeah. That was the strongest shit. How is that legal to make, let alone consume?"

"Daddy has a lot of time on his hands since he retired. He can't spend all of it fishin'. Though he been dabbling in 'shine 'bout as long as he's been doing his own beer. And since he don't sell it or nothing, it's all good."

I leaned closer to her and whispered, "Do I really have to finish it?" There wasn't much left in the jar, but I'd like to leave of my own accord rather than being carried off like a lightweight.

She lifted a shoulder and twisted her lips into a coy smile. "The man said you can't let good 'shine go to waste."

Before I could protest, she reached for the jar and downed the last of it like a shot, then slammed the empty container on the table. They all cheered and hollered. For half a second, I was ready to question my manhood if she could have handled it better than I had, but a thin line of perspiration formed above her upper lip, and she started fanning herself.

"Damn, Daddy. You changed it up?"

"Oh, yeah. Ya momma told me it needed a little more spice. Like her. And what my woman wants. My woman gets." With no shame or hesitation, he pulled his wife in for a kiss that could have almost turned exhibitionist if it had lasted any longer.

As the evening began to wind down, folks helped with clean-up before they headed home until it dwindled to just the four of us. Well two, since Regina and her mother had taken the last of the pots inside, leaving me with Mr. Charles.

"Take a walk with me, Alec."

Maybe I'd be getting those threats after all, but I fell into step with the older man. He was a stout guy with a bushy beard which was more black than gray. Which was unlike his hair that he wore in a micro fro even though it was thinning on top. He didn't come off as opposing as Sheriff Parker, but I knew better than to underestimate him all the same. "You have a nice piece of property out here."

"Yeah, yeah. We like it alright."

He didn't speak again until we'd reached the dock and he stared out at the dark water. Crickets chirped, subtle splashes could be heard of something jumping into the marsh. And the sky was clear with the stars sparkling bright as far as my eye could see. A peaceful location.

"You an adult. My Gina's an adult. I'm not one to get all up in the business. That's Mabel's job." He chuckled at his private joke. "But I will say, my girl has been stressed all to hell with the fire and all, and you seem to make it better for her."

I waited to see if more was to come, but it seemed as if he'd said his piece and was done. I attempted to formulate some reply, but the approach of the ladies kept any words firmly a jumbled mess in my brain.

"What you two out here discussing?" Regina asked.

"Oh, the usual don't hurt her or I'll chop you up and scatter your remains in the water."

Mrs. Charles slid one arm along his back and lightly slapped his chest. "Oh please. You have almost no bark and a nonexistent bite." Her teasing tone was followed up with a loving kiss to his cheek.

Regina slipped her hand into mine. "We should get going. You have a big day tomorrow, Special Investigator slash Trainer Hodge."

We said our goodbyes, and her parents escorted us to her car. They stayed in the driveway until we'd backed out. Time with her family had been an experience, and her parents reminded me a little of my own. A strong and loving relationship even after decades of marriage.

I turned my head toward her. "Does your father test every man you bring home by trying to burn them from the inside out?"

She cut her eyes over at me briefly. "You say every like you expect me to be traipsing men through my parents' house all the damn time."

I sat up a bit straighter in my seat. "That's not what I meant. I was curious what other tests might be in store."

She sighed heavily and tightened her grip on the steering wheel. "Can't say. Daddy's only pulled that stunt once before."

"And did he pass the test?" I wasn't so concerned with competing with some ex in the eyes of her family. The only opinion that really mattered to me was the woman in the driver's seat who was taking a long time to respond.

Another heavy sigh. "You could say that. I married him."

25

REGINA

I QUIETLY SANG ALONG TO ANITA BAKER AS I STOOD IN FRONT of my closet spending way too much time attempting to pick out outfits. It was two days, and it wasn't like I hadn't been out with Alec before. But this time...my doorbell chimed interrupting my thoughts.

"You have a key," I said by way of greeting to Cynthia.

"I know, but I'm not going to just walk up in your house unannounced."

I shut the door behind her. "Fair enough. Want anything to drink?"

"Nah, I'm good. I won't be staying long. Just wanted to check up on you."

I crossed my arms and frowned. "What for?"

She started to answer but stopped and whipped her head toward the hall. A slow smile grew as she began swaying to "You Bring Me Joy". "Whew, you got the mood music going."

"Not setting any mood, just packing, and all tasks are better when set to music." I headed back to my room with her trailing behind me singing.

My mini suitcase sat open in the middle of my bed, and it took her no time to pick up the emerald-green negligée that sat on top. The sheer lingerie was in a babydoll design with a ribbon of lace around the bust area that connected to hold it closed like a sash. It came with a pair of matching panties, equally as sheer. I loved wearing pretty underwear, and always as a set, but it'd been a long-ass time since I'd wanted to wear something sexy for someone other than myself.

"Not trying to set a mood, huh?" She arched a brow, and a teasing grin graced her face.

"Whatever." I turned back to my closet as she refolded the piece and returned it to the bag. "He hasn't been forthcoming with his plans, so I'm at a loss for what to pack. Do I need a dress for dinner? Or keep it casual for strolls on River Street or those ghost tours? Got me taking my ass to Savannah, but remaining mum on all other details." I huffed a breath before finally yanking my navy shirt dress from its hanger, along with a light cardigan.

"I'm glad you are finally doing this," Cynthia commented as she lounged on my bed.

I grabbed my black slacks, a bright yellow blouse, along with a pair of jeans and long-sleeved tee. "With everything I've had going on, and day away might be with the doctor ordered." I'd been going nonstop since the fire. Slowing down gave me too much time to think and worry and mentally kick my ass over how everything had fallen apart on my watch.

"Uh-huh. That's true. I'm more talking about you packing. As in you're staying the night instead of getting a fix then heading home."

I folded the outfits, then tossed the toiletry bag on top and zipped up my little overnight bag. I'd overthought the whole thing way too much since agreeing, and her comment brought back the cold feet. "I reserved a hotel room."

Cynthia sat up. "You didn't."

I shrugged.

"Does he know that?"

"Not exactly. Look, you and Irene were all 'give it a chance' and other such nonsense, and this is me doing it in my way. I am about to drive my ass to Savannah to go on what is quite possibly my first real date in years. Cut me some freakin' slack."

She sighed and rose from the bed. "I guess you're right. Baby steps and all that jazz." She put her hands on my shoulders and looked me directly in the eye. "But I'm proud of you. Happy for you. He makes you happy. I can tell. Hell, even Marcel picked up on it when we had dinner together." She hugged me tight. "I came by to make sure you hadn't talked yourself out of going completely. So, you booking a hotel to stay in your comfort zone, I'll take it."

I let her words cover me like a security blanket, holding the hope and possibilities in and keeping the doubt and negative thoughts at bay. Momma and Tricia were holding down the catering at the B&B for the weekend, sending me off with their unasked for blessings. With Cynthia here and practically shoving me out the door to my own damn house, I had no excuse not to go and attempt to enjoy myself. *Attempt*...I was straight lying to myself. A bigger part of me was looking forward to time spent with Alec, whether I wanted to admit it or not.

❧

THE CLOSER I got to the city, the more my heart raced. And with my arrival, I worried it would beat clean out of my chest. I kept replaying things in my head. How Alec was so intent on dating me. How he made me feel cared for and cared about. How my father had tested him the same way he'd done Lawrence.

Daddy... He was a man of few words, never got into my personal life unless I asked for the most part, but even he'd given his blessing of sorts. I sucked in a breath, remembering how he said he was happy I had found another good man. A man who so obviously adored me.

I pulled into the parking lot of the Savannah Fire Department and whipped into one of the visitor spaces, then killed the engine. All the pep talks I'd given to myself and the words Cynthia had spoken just an hour prior flew out the window.

How in the hell did I let Alec talk me into this? Going on dates was one thing, but he'd asked me to spend the weekend with him. The weekend. This was not what I did. This was not who I was. But as I climbed out of my SUV and headed into the station in search of him to get his keys, it was what I was doing. I was picking up his keys, since he wasn't off for a few more hours, and he said I could let myself into his house as if it was the most natural thing in the world to do, instead of checking into the hotel I had waiting.

"Can I help you, miss?" A tall, somewhat muscular woman with short locs pulled back into a low ponytail greeted me as I entered the building and she climbed out of a truck.

"Yes. I'm looking for Alec Hodge."

She smiled before turning to bellow out, "Hodge. You got a visitor."

A few others popped their heads out, and a chain reaction of them all hollering for him went off.

She turned back to me and held her hand out. "I'm Sasha, by the way. You a friend of his?"

I juggled the foil container in my arms to shake her hand. "Yeah. Something like that."

She looked me up and down, and the grin on her face got wider. "Ah. My loss. He should be out shortly." Sasha held on to me for another half a beat before letting go and went back to whatever she'd been doing on the truck.

I glanced around the station, which was at least twice the size of the one back home. A few moments later, he came strolling forward, and a large smile stretched across his face when he saw me.

"There's my lady, looking fine as ever."

Thoughts flipped through my head like rapid fire at his statement. The use of "my lady" and all the implications it entailed.

However, when he tilted my chin up for a quick kiss, none of it seemed to matter.

"Hey, yourself. I brought treats." I stepped back and held up the container.

"Oh, you will win over the guys real quick with these. Yo, Sasha," he called over his shoulder. "Especially with her. She eats and drinks most of us under the table," he whispered.

"What up?"

He handed her the foil tray. "Regina is the best baker I know and brought us stuff."

She lifted the lid and peeked inside at the variety of options. "I'm supposed to share these? Y'all gonna have to fight me for them." Her crooked grin made me laugh.

"I have a feeling you'd be the victor."

She winked at me. "No doubt."

Alec looked back and forth between the two of us, but before he could make any comment an alarm blared. The container was thrust back into my hands, and guys came running out of nowhere.

"Shit. Um, the keys. See the chief and he'll get them out of my locker." Alec quickly kissed me on the cheek before he ran off to join the others, who were all suiting up.

He was suiting up.

I pressed back against the wall as everything happened in slow motion. Shouts, running, that damn alarm blaring and seemingly getting louder with each wail.

He was suiting up.

Alec was an investigator. That was his title. Special Investigator. Yet he was rushing around and hopping onto one of the engines heading off to a fire.

No.

The trucks roared past me as they rolled out to save the day for someone. I stood frozen against the wall with my heart lodged in my throat.

Even after the madness was over and the building had gone

silent, I couldn't move. My ears continued to ring, and my heart raced.

He'd suited up.

"Miss?"

I blinked and focused on an older gentleman standing in front of me.

"You look almost pale. Being that up close when a call comes in can be a bit frightening. Let's get you over to the bench so you can take a seat."

I shook my head quickly. "I...I'm okay. I...I need to go." Absentmindedly, I handed him the tray then willed my legs to carry me out to my car.

"I don't know if you should drive right now," he called out to me, but I kept walking.

My hands shook, and I dropped my keys twice before I managed to unlock the door and climb inside. I rested my head against the steering wheel, squeezing it with my hands while taking large gulps of air.

I knew better. I fucking knew better. I didn't get involved. I didn't let myself get invested. And I sure as hell didn't let myself care. The shaking started to subside, and I sat up straight. I didn't care. I wasn't invested. And I wouldn't worry about his safety. By the time I made it home, I hopefully would almost believe it.

26

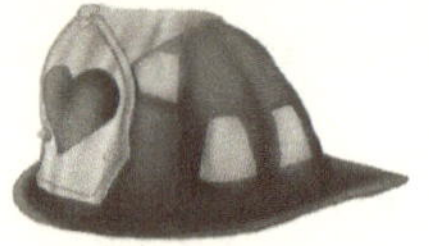

ALEC

I KNOCKED ON THE DOOR TO THE CHIEF'S OFFICE BEFORE popping my head in. A half-eaten brownie sat on his desk. Four more hours, and then I had two glorious days with Regina.

"Hey, boss. Thanks for getting Regina my keys."

He frowned and barely glanced up from the computer. "The lady with the great desserts? She didn't ask me for any keys. Hightailed it out of here right after y'all rolled out."

"Oh..."

He cracked his neck. "Yeah. She seemed a bit spooked with the alarm and everything."

I tapped the doorframe with my fist twice. "Thanks."

I took the stairs two at a time up to my bunk. Sure enough, my keys sat on top next to my phone. I grabbed the device then dialed her number. It rang. And rang. And rang until her voicemail picked up. I disconnected because I didn't want to leave a message with prying ears around. But she'd left. Why in the hell would she run off?

For the rest of the night, I tried and failed to get Regina on the phone. My voicemails and texts went unanswered, and I got antsier as a result. Chief said she'd been upset. What if something had happened to her? What if she'd gotten into an accident? I spent the rest of my shift unsettled and mostly watching the damn clock until I was off.

I was out of the door and in my Jeep by 8:05. I'd expected to go home and spend the night with Regina, instead, after a seventy-two-hour shift, I was heading down I-516 toward Madison Island after a quick stop to back a bag. Pure adrenaline kept my eyes open during the drive, which spiked when I got to the bridge with the welcome sign. I squeezed the steering wheel as I cruised through the sleepy town toward her house.

When I pulled into the driveway, the windows were mostly dark, but there was a little light shining through. I practically ran to the front door and rang the bell. No answer. I rang it again two more times. Still no answer.

"Regina," I yelled, banging on the door.

The front porch lights of her neighbors flicked on, and when I turned to the left, I saw the curtains moving in one of the windows of their house. It might have been crazy, but I needed to see her. I needed to find out what the hell happened. Why wasn't she taking my calls?

I banged on the door again. "Regina, why won't you answer me?"

I moved to the window and cupped my hands against the glass to peer in. I couldn't see any movement. Continuing to the side of the house, I repeated my actions, hoping to catch the slightest indication that she was in there but simply hiding out for some reason. Over and over in my head I attempted to figure out what happened and came up empty.

The sound of a car door got my attention.

"You're making quite the ruckus, son," Sheriff Parker said, approaching me.

Small towns. Her neighbors had called the damn police. Shit. But he wasn't in uniform, nor was he driving an official car. And he was her father-in-law, of sorts. Fucking hell, this couldn't be worse.

"Evenin', Sheriff. I just needed to talk to her."

"Yeah. Apparently, the whole neighborhood is aware of that. But don't look like she's home." He spun his keys around his finger as he stared me down. "What's so urgent you need to go beating on her door like a bill collector in the middle of the night?"

Middle of the night? It was barely past nine. But, small towns.

I took a breath to calm my annoyance. "I just needed to make sure she was okay."

His demeanor changed as he straightened to draw out his height and his brows furrowed together as she stared at me. "Why wouldn't she be? You do something to her?"

I swallowed and shook my head. "Not at all. We had plans for the weekend, sir, then we got a call at the station, and she just left."

"Got a call?"

I took another breath to keep myself in check. "Yes, sir. Had to go out for a fire."

He visibly relaxed and went back to spinning his keys and made a humph noise. "Well, come on in. I don't think she's home, but I'll call her."

I stepped to the side as he unlocked the door and let me in. The house was eerily quiet, and it felt wrong to be in her space without her. But he'd let me in, so hopefully he'd take the heat for this.

"Have a seat." He pointed toward the couch as he closed the door behind him.

I sat in one of the side chairs and ran my hands down my thighs. I was tired and anxious. And alone with the father of her deceased husband. The sheriff whipped out his phone—a flip phone—then squinted as he stabbed at the buttons. I watched him as he paced back and forth.

"Hey, Gigi. Look I'm over at your house. No...nothing's wrong. Just that young fella. The fire inspector was here, and the neighbors called it in. No, he didn't break in, he was just lookin' for you. No, I didn't tell him to leave, we're here waiting. Yes, I let him in."

He pulled the phone away from his ear, and although I couldn't make out what she was saying, I could tell she wasn't happy.

"Because I did. No. Just get yourself home. Well, have Cynthia or Marcel drive you, but get over here." He laughed as more yelling came through the phone. I did catch something about her taking back the key. He simply laughed and said "see you soon" before hanging up.

"Welp, son, I hope you know what you're doin' because she's madder than hell right now. Mostly at me because I let you in, but you're gonna take the heat."

"It's fine. I can handle it."

He took a seat on the sofa and stared at me. "Can you?"

It felt like he was sizing me up. Maybe doing a mental comparison between me and his son. I didn't know the particulars surrounding his death. It was a topic Regina hadn't brought back up. But it was clear that regardless of how long her husband had been gone, the relationship she had with the man in front of me had remained intact. It didn't matter. One thing had become abundantly clear to me during my mad dash to find her, I had fallen hard for Regina Parker.

I wanted to be with her. To take care of her...as much as she'd let me. But I wanted her, in all her stubborn and independent glory. And I was willing to do whatever it took to make that happen.

I loved her.

I looked at Sheriff Parker and nodded. "Yes, sir. I can. And will."

He huffed a laugh. "Alright then."

Car doors slamming got our attention. I jumped up from the chair and headed over to open the door. She stopped when she saw me, a frown deepening her features. Marcel stood behind her with his wife, and a sympathetic smile on his face.

"Why are you here?" Regina snapped, eyes narrowed as she glared at me.

"Because you wouldn't answer the damn phone."

"That would indicate I didn't want to talk to you."

"Possibly, but I'm here so no getting around it now."

Her frown deepened, and her razor-sharp gaze moved from me to her father-in-law as he stepped up beside me. She pointed a finger at him. "You. How are you just gonna let him into my house? Why didn't you run him off?"

He moved closer and kissed her cheek. "Because. Now, I gotta get back. Lucille is waiting for me."

She startled back. "Ms. Lucille. Waiting...what?"

"Gigi, you not the only one that can keep your business out of the gossip mill." He nodded slowly. "Or at least you did. Now...not so much," he added with a smile before turning to pat my shoulder. "Good luck."

There was a look, more secret communication that exchanged between them, like at the pizzeria with the waitress. The sheriff said his goodbyes to Marcel and Cynthia, then ambled out to his car.

Cynthia approached Regina and gave her a hug. "I'll come get you in the morning so you can get your car. Or...you can have Alec drive you. And remember what we said." She smiled at me. "Have a good night, Alec."

Marcel nodded and held his wife's hand as they walked away.

Regina crossed her arms and tilted her head toward the door. "You can go, too."

I reached forward and shut the door. "I could, but I'm not."

"Ain't this a bitch? Everybody just up and thinks they know better than me what I need or want."

She stormed off toward her kitchen, continuing to cuss and fuss. It was going to be a long night, but at least she wasn't trying to throw me out.

27

REGINA

I OPENED THE CABINET TO GET A GLASS AND WAS PISSED THE soft close mechanism prevented me from being able to slam it. He had a lot of nerve showing up here. And Pops. I could not believe that man let Alec into my house. That was not why he still had a key. Emergencies only. Alec Hodge mad he would have blue balls for the weekend did not constitute an emergency.

The devil in question strolled in and took a seat at the island as if he had every right to be in my house. In my life. In my heart. I paused and rested my palms against the cool granite. Damn him. Damn him straight to hell. But it wasn't going to work.

"Why are you here, Alec?"

"Why did you leave, Regina?"

I took in a breath as I moved over to the fridge and filled my glass with water. I drank it slow, keeping my back to the man who had somehow managed to upend my being. My equilibrium was off because of him, and the only way to stop the tilt was to send him on his way.

Nerves somewhat steady, I turned to face him. "I left because I realized whatever this was had run its course."

"Bullshit. If that was the case, you wouldn't have shown up to begin with. We spent a week making these plans. You were fully on board, and you just up and ditch. Makes no sense."

I slammed the glass down. "It doesn't have to make sense. I changed my damn mind."

He shot up from his chair. "Again, bullshit. What the hell happened?"

"What makes you think anything did?"

He huffed a laugh. "Mainly because you won't answer the fucking question. If it's one thing I'm sure of about you, Regina, it's that you always say what you want to say. Yet you're doing the two-step."

Alec glared at me, not backing down. Not that I expected him to. He'd blown up my phone and text messages. When Pops called to say Alec was here, I knew I couldn't avoid him, but that didn't mean I didn't hold on to a sliver of hope that he'd simply take my answer and go.

My comeback that he didn't know shit about me lodged in my throat. I'd done this to myself. Somehow, I'd let my guard down around Alec Hodge, and now I was paying the price. I stared at him, dressed in his black cargo pants and SFD T-shirt. An outfit similar to what he'd worn the first day he'd blown into my life. What he'd worn when he'd been introduced as Special Investigator.

I walked over to the kitchen table and collapsed in one of the chairs. The weariness of everything once again catching up to me. "I can't do it."

"Do what?" All previous traces of frustration vanished from his tone as he picked up a chair and sat right in front of me.

His face softened, and the hints of caring and understanding seeped in. The very thing that had me in this predicament to begin with.

"All this time I thought you were an investigator. *Only* an investigator."

"This...this is about my job?" He scrubbed his hands down

his face. "I've been racking my brain trying to figure out what I may have done and it's just my job."

"There is no 'just' to this, *not* Special Investigator Hodge. I..." I ran my tongue along the front of my teeth and got up to pace.

This was not a topic I discussed. Those that knew me understood. I never wanted to embark on the conversation that loomed ahead of me. I never thought I'd have to. The lifestyle changes I'd made were to ensure I wouldn't end up in the same situation. Once was plenty.

Alec wrapped his fingers around my wrist. "The danger aspect worries you?"

"Terrifies would be a better word."

He slipped his arm around my waist, and I didn't want to acknowledge how good his embrace was. Or how much I needed to be held. How much I needed *him* to hold me.

"Look, I get it. When I told my parents what I was going to do, my mom all but freaked out. She still wants me to have a desk job. And I'm sort of working on that, but honestly I love what I do."

I pulled free. "And that's why this won't work. I can't...I've buried one man I lo— I've buried one man, and that was due to an accident. What should have been a fun filled day ended with the loss of my husband and mother-in-law and the near loss of my son. I'm not about to play Russian Roulette with someone that purposefully runs headfirst into danger."

My heart squeezed. Somewhere along the lines, I'd not simply let Alec in, but I'd foolishly gone and fallen in love with him. A man that put his life on the line each time he suited up. His profession was noble. Heroic even, but I couldn't... There was no way I could sit around every day he left for work wondering if I'd get a knock on my door again.

His troublemaking, sexy grin spread across his face. "Ms. Regina Parker, you care about me."

I planted my hands on my hips. "That's your takeaway?"

Once again, I was enclosed in his embrace. "No. My takeaway is that you're scared. You suffered a loss. A major loss, and you're wanting to avoid experiencing that level of pain again." He spoke softly, his voice soothing the raw wounds that had been reopened.

I swallowed the lump in my throat. "It's been sixteen years, yet some days it hurts like it was yesterday," I whispered.

No more pretending or avoiding. I was too tired to keep playing the dodge game. I'd already opened the door to reveal the truth behind it. Alec led us over to the couch but kept me secured in his arms as we sat.

"You're a good man, Alec. And despite my best efforts... Doesn't matter. I can't put myself in a position where tragedy is almost a guarantee."

He placed his fingers under my chin and made me look at him. "Regina, I've been a firefighter for over ten years and never gotten so much as a scratch."

"Doesn't mean it won't happen. There's risk in the every day, I know that, understand that, but that risk is compounded by your job."

He sat up, closed his eyes, and sighed. "What do you want me to do?"

"Nothing."

"I don't accept that. Regina. This. Us. I'm not ready to let it go. You leaving like you did, and not answering my calls. I was out of my fucking mind with worry. First, that maybe something happened to you. Then I thought I'd somehow, some way done something to fuck up."

He rested his forehead against mine and ran his thumb along my cheek. "I need you, Regina Parker. In a way I've never needed or wanted anyone in my life. You are always on my mind. Always. All the stress you have going on with your bakery. That fucker that burned it down. The food truck. I want to take it away. I actively think of ways I can lessen that burden. I want to be part of your world. Your inner circle. Someone you know without a doubt has your back and you can depend on.

We are good together, Regina. Don't let that go. I'm begging you."

His stare was piercing. Those dark-brown eyes gazed deep into my soul. His pleading, heartfelt words sang to the part of me that died sixteen years prior. The part of me that basked in the commitment. The part of me that longed for everything he offered. To have someone to share the highs and lows with.

"Why?" My throat was dry, scratchy, but I forced the question past my lips.

Why now? Why this man? So many whys to be asked. I'd actively avoided this for so long, and it'd snuck up on me and smacked me in the face.

A sly grin lifted the corner of his mouth. "Isn't it obvious, Ms. Parker? I'm in love with you."

His answer knocked the air from my lungs. I placed a shaky hand on his cheek and pressed my lips to his. Soft at first, but the passion quickly grew. I swept my tongue through his mouth and leaned into his strong embrace. Alec gave as good as he got, holding the back of my neck as he deepened the kiss, our lips moving at a feverous pace. I didn't know if it was the wine I'd consumed or the clean, warm scent of Alec that made my head swim, but I was dizzy. Dizzy on the possibilities. Dizzy on the hope and wonder. Dizzy on all the things I'd denied myself over the years that now sat right in front of me. It was risky, and terrifying, but I wanted it. I wanted him.

I pulled away and took in gulps of air. The last barrier. My final line remained between us.

"Will you stay the night?"

He nodded. "Let me go get my bag out the Jeep."

"You came prepared?"

He lifted a shoulder. "I was hopeful."

I turned out the lights and waited by the door for Alec to return. I dropped my gaze to the gray overnight bag in his hand, then laced our fingers and led us down the hall. Crossing the threshold with Alec in tow kicked my heartbeat up. I waged a silent internal battle. The room and furniture had changed over the years, yet it had remained sacred in a way. Alec brought our joined hands to his lips and pressed a kiss to the back of mine before easily strolling over to the club chair in the corner.

Tonight, that all changed. I swallowed down the dryness in my mouth and went about my bedtime routine as if it were any other night. As if the man taking off his boots hadn't professed his love for me, and I was left barreling full speed downhill with no brakes into territory I'd put off limits long ago.

When I exited the bathroom with my locs secured in a wrap and my comfy nightgown on, I found Alec sitting on the bed waiting. He'd turned off the overhead light so only the lamp remained on and gave off a soft glow.

"Don't know which side is yours." A lopsided grin quirked up the corner of his mouth.

"All of it, but I'll be generous and let you take the right."

He stood and pulled the covers back. "Opposed to?"

"Making you sleep in the chair."

He laughed quietly and shook his head as he climbed into my king, holding his arm out for me to join him. As I settled down beside him, the storming seas calmed. He reached over me to turn off the lamp then cocooned me in his arms. I closed my eyes. A low sigh of contentment escaped my lips as I relaxed into his strong embrace. For the first time in sixteen years, I was going to sleep with a man, and I was ecstatic about it.

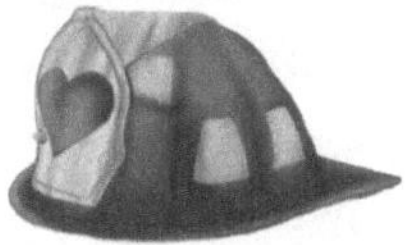

❧ 28 ❧

REGINA

MY EYES FLUTTERED OPEN, AND I SQUEEZED THEM SHUT against the intruding sunlight. Squinting, I slowly opened them again, and the more I became conscious to the day, the more the events of last night came flooding back. I turned my head to the side to find the bed empty. Had he left? After everything, the thought momentarily made my blood run cold.

I pushed into a seated position and spotted his pants in a clump on the floor next to his overnight bag. A rush of relief flooded me. I'd let him stay. I'd asked him to stay. The tilt of my universe was more severe than ever.

Pushing off the bed, I headed to the bathroom. As I brushed my teeth, I focused on the small black toiletry bag next to the second sink, which had largely been unused for years. I had to deal with a morning-after conversation, and we didn't even have sex. He'd held me. I'd fallen asleep in the arms of a man for the first time in sixteen long years. I didn't think it would be possible, but as I'd laid next to Alec's warm body, I'd drifted into the most peaceful sleep I'd had since the fire. When I entered my bedroom again, Alec stood in boxer briefs, holding a plate and a coffee mug and wearing a large grin.

"Good morning."

I blinked once. Then twice. And a third time. "You cooked?"

"Don't sound so shocked. My mom wanted to make sure we left her house knowing how to take care of ourselves. I can cook. Clean. And iron with military precision."

He inclined his head toward the bed, and somehow my feet carried me over.

"I told you last night I wanted to take care of you. And I meant every word. So, you have a ham and cheese omelet with a few bell peppers mixed in, sausage patties, and coffee."

Too many thoughts swirled in my head as I stared at the plate. He'd gotten up and fixed me breakfast. And it looked edible. Not a burnt bit in sight. *He'd cooked me breakfast.*

"Thank you," I whispered, still staring at the plate. I was in over my head. Digging a deeper hole with each passing second. While last night was great, it was a momentary illusion. The reason I'd ran and the main reason it wouldn't work remained a factor to be dealt with.

He crawled up behind me, propped up on his elbow, and rested his other hand on my hip. I shoved a forkful of egg into my mouth and moaned when the fluffy bite hit my tongue. Damn, he really could cook.

"Good, huh?"

I swallowed and fought back a smile. "It's alright."

"Uh-huh. I know something else that can make you moan like that, and I know it's way better than just 'alright'."

I shook my head and couldn't hold back the laugh. This was all surreal. So out of the ordinary, but oddly familiar and comfortable all the same.

He opened and closed his fingers along my back. A simple action, but it was enough to cause goosebumps to spring up along my arms. "What are our plans for the day?"

"I don't have any since I was supposed to be in Savannah."

Alec inched closer and pressed his lips to the back of my arm. "I'm down to stay in bed all day."

I glanced over my shoulder at him. "Is that so?"

"That omelet is full of protein, so that means you should have plenty of energy. And since we are already at your house, no running out on me."

I forced the bite of sausage past the lump that quickly formed at his statement and had to take a sip of coffee to wash it down.

I set the plate on the nightstand then twisted to look at him. Reaching out, I cupped his cheek, and the whiskers of his beard scratched the palm of my hand. "It wasn't running out. I simply preferred to sleep in my own bed. Alone. I've not slept with anyone...since..."

He sat up. "You mean as in sleep, sleep?"

I nodded. He wrapped his arms around my waist, and I yelped when he flipped us so that he had me pinned beneath him.

"Thank you."

I drew my brows together. "For what?"

"Trusting me. Letting me in. Not running from what has to be a lot of emotional change. I know you are strong and pride yourself on your independence. But you let the wall down."

I had, but it was all for naught. "Alec, what I said last night. Nothing's changed."

He kissed my neck and trailed his fingers up my outer thigh. "Everything's changed," he replied in a husky whisper.

He slid his hand between my legs and cupped my pussy, using his palm to press against me. A move that stole my breath and scrambled my thoughts.

"Alec..."

He leaned up to stare at me, rolling his tongue between his full, kissable lips while slipping his hand beneath the waistband of my panties. "Let me make love to you, Regina. And afterward, I'll hold you and explain how we're going to be okay. I promise."

He slowly stroked me, softly teasing my clit while keeping his gaze firmly locked on mine. He was so sure we'd be okay. That we would even be a "we." The doubts and worries danced in the back of my mind, but I wanted the dream. The possibility. Despite my lingering fears, I wanted him.

Reaching up, I pulled his head closer and dropped my legs wider. I stopped fighting the battle. I surrendered.

Alec kissed me. His soft lips moving atop mine slowly, as if getting acquainted with them for the first time. I opened my mouth, letting his tongue inside, gripping the back of his head to hold him to me. The hand between my legs continued to stroke and tease.

His palm pressing against me moved in slow, deliberate circles as he slid his fingers into my body. This man was in love with me. He'd given me something I thought I'd never have again. Something I'd told myself I never wanted or needed again.

Alec kept caressing me. Unrushed in his actions. Inching me closer and closer to the edge. "You are beautiful," he whispered against my lips. "You are beautiful and strong. Vulnerable, yet independent. And mine." As he spoke, Alec continued to move his fingers in and out of my body at his leisurely pace.

I rocked my hips, matching his movements. His erection was a rock against my thigh, thick and hard, and it added to the short circuiting of my brain as he continued his expert fondling.

He pressed his lips to the side of my neck, planting light kisses up until he nipped at my earlobe. "I'm going to love you. Take care of you. And make it my absolute mission to blow your back out at every opportunity."

I choked on the laugh that lodged in my throat as the orgasm he'd been leading me toward slammed into me. I grabbed his bicep and squeezed my eyes shut while the waves of bliss lapped over me. Alec kept his motions slow and steady, riding out my release while continuing to pepper my neck and face with light kisses. He didn't stop. Alec circled my clit with his thumb while he lowered his head to suck my nipple through the thin fabric of my gown.

This man should not have made my body feel as good as he did. I worked my hand down to grasp his dick and he moaned at the contact. I stroked him as slowly as he fucked me with his fingers. Moving down his length then up again. I realized in that moment I'd never touched him, and I'd been missing out. The heaviness of his cock in my hand was joyous.

Alec applied more pressure to my sensitive nub, winding the cord tighter and tighter until I was arching off the bed as my stomach clenched from the pleasure.

"That's it, baby. Give it all to me," he huskily commanded before claiming my lips.

My heart raced, air caught in my lungs, and my entire being shuddered from the aftershocks.

"Where do you keep your condoms?" he whispered the question, his breath almost cool against my heated skin.

Unable to form words, I turned my head toward the bathroom.

"Be right back." He hopped off the bed, a large, obvious tent to the front of his black boxer briefs.

I tugged my gown over my head and had wiggled out of my damp panties by the time he returned.

He paused and raked his eyes over my naked body, and I did the same to him.

"I'm a lucky, lucky man," he said, slowing his stroll.

The appreciation...the love in his dark eyes made me shudder. "That you are." And I didn't do so bad myself, but I didn't voice those words.

His impressive latex-covered dick stood out, hard and ready for action. I licked my lips, I'd not yet had a chance to taste him. A misstep I needed to rectify because nothing would have delighted me more than to hear how high of a pitch he'd squeal as I swallowed him. He set the box on the nightstand next to my unfinished breakfast.

"All of them?

He settled on top of me with his signature grin in place. "I told you. In bed. All. Damn. Day." He accented each word with a peck to my mouth as he nudged my legs wider. He'd been hopeful of that last time, only now I was almost obliged to let him give it his best shot.

When he pushed forward, we moaned in unison. I glided my hands up his back, enjoying the ripples of his muscles beneath my touch. Alec pulled back and eased in again slowly. His unrushed pace and the deep gaze into my eyes stole my breath. We found a tempo. Alec was in no hurry. He made love to me with gentle, deep strokes and passionate kisses. Each thrust pushing me further and further away from the reasons why we wouldn't work.

I arched my back and raked my nails down his. His hard body rubbing against mine, driving me closer to a most pleasurable destination. And I was primed and ready to take the trip.

Alec squeezed my thigh. "On top. I want the best seat in the house when you come."

Positions switched, Alec palmed my breasts. He circled his thumbs around my erect nipples, the simple action acting like a string being yanked tight, making me clench around him.

Hands on his chest, I rotated my hips, an easy move to stick with the pace he'd set. He filled me. Stretched me. Loved me. I closed my eyes at the last thought and lifted up then sank back down on his thick shaft. Mutual groans poured free. The thumps of his heartbeat increased beneath my touch.

Alec grabbed my ass, bent his knees, and lifted his hips, driving himself deeper. My breathing increased to match the speed. I leaned forward, and once again our lips were joined in the hedonistic dance our bodies were entangled in. Moans grew louder, mingling with the slapping of flesh and huffs of ragged breaths.

I rode him, gliding up and down on his dick. Smooth caresses against my aroused walls, friction on my swollen clit, and his warm hands guiding my movements. Every inch of me acutely aware of Alec, yet somehow it wasn't enough. My pace increased, and he met me thrust for thrust.

"Yeah, baby. Come on. Give it to me," he ground out, smacking my ass.

The bed squeaked, sweat coated our bodies. My nipples scraped across his chest with each rock of my hips, an added sensation fueling my chase for utopia.

Alec craned his neck back. "Fuck!" The strangled word pinged around in my head.

He gripped my ass and thrust up again. Heat bloomed within me as he came and my own release broke free, shooting through me like lightning, electrifying my senses and sending me free-falling into a most welcomed oblivion. I rested my head on his shoulder as the aftershocks zinged to a stop.

Alec wrapped his arms around me and held me tight. His heavy breaths blew across my heated, dewy skin. As the fog began to lift, his quiet comfort lulled yet terrified me.

ALEC

I glanced around Regina's room while she finished her shower. I'd wanted to join her, but she'd turned me down, saying there would be no more distraction sex until after we talked. On her dresser was a small grouping of pictures. The largest one was of Regina and a man, it looked to be a wedding picture. Her dreads were much shorter, and a brown which matched... I shook off the comparison and picked up the frame. Her smile was radiant, and her husband's expression held such adoration as his frozen image gazed upon her.

I wasn't one to compare myself to others, or feel the need to compete, but from the photograph alone, I suddenly felt like I had big shoes to fill. I returned the frame to its place. The rest of the grouping all seemed to contain him. A shot of them in the hospital holding their son. Him and the then little boy on a beach, sitting beside a small sandcastle. The pictures she had on her mantel were more recent. Most of them with her and her friends. Or her with her son. His graduation picture taking center stage. But the ones she kept in her room... Regina Parker in another life.

I turned to face the disheveled bed. Sex. That had been an activity Regina could separate her emotions from. But the intimacy of sleeping with someone, she'd closed that off. Until last night. The water shut off, and I took a seat to wait. A few minutes later, the door opened, and a billowing of steam poured into the room.

"Holy shit. You scared me." Regina clutched at her chest—her naked chest—as she strolled out wearing nothing more than her birthday suit.

"Where else was I supposed to be?"

"I don't know, in the living room. Maybe cleaning up whatever mess you left in my kitchen."

I moved back, rolling to my side and resting my head on my fist, clocking her movements around the room and fully enjoying the sight of her bare form. "And miss this show? Never. Besides, I didn't leave a mess. Told you I can cook *and* clean."

Regina sat on the bed and began rubbing lotion on to her leg. She was in no hurry. No rush to dress. Confident and beautiful in her nudeness. I moved to kneel before her and grabbed the bottle, pumping three squirts of the moisturizer into my hand. She kept her eyes on me as I took over the duties. Rubbing and caressing her leg, giving her a gentle massage in the process.

"Told you no more sex until after we talk," she commented as I moved my hands higher.

I added more lotion to my palm. "I'm not trying to have sex with you. This is me keeping my word and taking care of you."

"I don't need anyone to take care of me." She said the words, but her eyes closed as I kneaded the ball of her foot.

"What if I want to? What if I want to rub your feet at the end of a long day? What if I want to listen to you complain about any and everything? Maybe you think you don't need anyone to take care of you, but you have me here applying for the job anyway."

She glanced down at me, her light brown eyes saying all the words she wouldn't verbalize. "Alec, please let me get dressed. I'll be out in a moment."

I pressed my lips together and swallowed down my objection.

Placing my hands on my thighs, I pushed myself to standing. "I'll be in the living room."

I closed her bedroom door behind me and wandered down the hall. I took a seat in the center of her couch and waited. Leaning my head back, I closed my eyes and started formulating a speech. Convincing her my job wasn't the death sentence she feared it to be. Fuck, I couldn't begin to imagine the loss she'd suffered. And it'd had a lasting effect on her. One I was up against. But she was worth it.

"I wear you out?"

I sat up and was met with her playful, flirtatious grin.

"You did, but I've got my second wind now."

"I'm sure you do.

I'd hoped she would have joined me on the couch. Instead, she got comfortable in the very chair I'd been in last night.

She tucked her feet under the butt and waved her hand as if presenting something. "Alright, you said you'd explain how this is supposed to work. Get to talking."

"I also said I'd hold you, but you're way over there."

She pushed her colorless lips out into a small pout and shook her head. "And Imma stay over here."

Scooting to the edge of the cushion, I rubbed my hands on my thighs. Regina wasn't known for making things easy on me. Not sure why I'd expected the current situation to be any different.

"Will you tell me about him?"

"About who?"

"Your husband."

Her eyes went wide before she furrowed her brow in a deep frown. "What does Lawrence have to do with us?"

Lawrence... I rolled his name around in my head for a moment, knowing I needed to tread carefully. "Because what you had with him. More importantly, how you lost him colors how you see me, my job, and our viability as a couple."

She turned away from me and glanced down the empty hallway. In her side profile I again was given a glimpse of the hidden part of Regina. When the facade dropped and she wasn't presenting the strong, lively, and quick-witted part of her personality. I'd learned that Regina didn't want to be seen as vulnerable...she didn't want to be seen as weak.

"The time you thought about moving away was after he died, wasn't it?"

Her eyes fluttered closed, and the deep inhale and slow exhale were answer enough. When she turned back to look at me, the glimpse had come to a close. "But I didn't because this is my home. It's all I know, and it's really all I want to know. And your job aside, you've said plenty that small-town life isn't for you. So, impasse either way."

I stood to cross the short distance to her. "Move over." As I spoke, I wiggled my ass down and squeezed myself in beside her on the oversized chair.

"What in the hell are you doing? I have too much hip and ass to be sitting with you in this chair." She complained but moved to give me space.

"There, this is better," I sighed. "We fit perfectly. Like we're meant to be." I stretched my arm around her shoulders.

She frowned at me but didn't resist.

I stroked her cheek. "Do you want to be with me? With all factors out of the way, would you want us?"

"It's not that easy."

"Answer the question."

She huffed out an annoyed breath. "Yes. There. Happy?"

"Ecstatic. And you're right, living in a small town would not have been something I'd have ever pictured myself doing. Until I met an amazing woman who gives me hell for sport, and I love every minute of it. I love her." I leaned and kissed her softly. "I love you, Regina Parker, and if you wanted to live in an igloo in the middle of the arctic, I'd ask when we're moving."

She covered her face and started laughing. It wasn't exactly the reaction I'd expected.

"Oh, Special Investigator, that was a great line. It was. And at least there'd be no fires for you to rush off to in the middle of the arctic."

"What if I took a desk job? Of sorts."

"Do you love what you do?"

"Yes."

"Then I couldn't ask you to give it up. I wouldn't make you choose."

"I know. And you're not. Becoming an investigator already has me on a path to be off the truck. I knew that when I made the decision to become one. And your fire chief has been working on recruiting me. He wants to retire for real." I kissed her again. "I've been considering it. You, Regina Parker, are all the excitement in my life that I need. A much bigger adrenaline rush than running into a fire. I just need to know you want me."

My heart raced and worry bubbled in my gut. Never had I laid out my feelings like I had for her. Never had I wanted to. And with each passing second, cracks in my confidence formed. She opened her mouth to speak, but whatever she was about to say was cut off by the sound of keys in the lock.

❧ 30 ❧

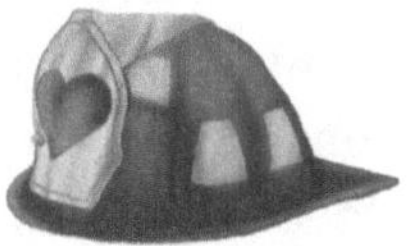

ALEC

"Hey, Mo—" Regina's son stopped mid-sentence when he laid eyes on us. "Oh...maybe I should have called first."

He slowly shut the door after a tall, slender young lady walked in behind him. Regina untangled herself from me, her body language changing as she headed over to her son. My stomach remained in knots with the unanswered declaration hanging in the air. But as she greeted her son, I appeared to be the only one bothered. And since I was the only one who had put themselves out, I supposed it fit. I pushed down my disappointment. It would have to wait for another time.

"Baby, this is a great surprise." She hugged him, then turned her attention to his companion. "And you brought Shonda," she said with an elevated pitch, giving the woman just as warm of an embrace.

Her son kept his eyes on me when he spoke. "Yeah. Shonda thought it might be nice to surprise you since I haven't come to visit lately."

Regina followed his line of sight. "Darnell, you remember Alec, right? He was the investigator Chief Morris brought in."

I stood and held my hand out. He looked me up and down before shaking it.

"Good to see you again. In my house. In the morning. With my mom."

"Boy, stop. It's nearly twelve." She turned to me. "Alec, this is Shonda, Darnell's girlfriend."

"Nice to meet you," Shonda said, her eyes darting from me to Regina and back again, a slow smile spreading across her face.

"You two hungry? Let me whip you up something to eat."

Regina easily slipped into maternal mode and showed yet another side to her personality. One that acted as another realization I'd not thought about. Yes, she had a child, but since he wasn't around, I was ashamed to admit that he hadn't factored into my grand scheme.

He ignored her question and directed one of his own at me. "I thought the investigation was over. Mom said the construction was under way."

I kept the grin from forming. I didn't know who was worse, the son, the father-in-law, or her father? But the son...Darnell. She'd lost her husband, and he'd lost a father. No doubt that meant the bond between mother and son was a tight one.

"It is and it has." I glanced at Regina, then back to Darnell. "This is more of a social call."

Regina walked over to her son and placed a hand on his arm. "Go to the table. Shonda, can you give us a minute?"

"Yes, ma'am." The young lady smiled at her boyfriend, then at me before heading down the hall to the bedrooms.

"Um...I'll let you two talk," I said, ready to follow Shonda's lead, but Regina grabbed my hand. A move that didn't go unnoticed by Darnell.

"This is serious then?" he asked.

"Go sit. Alec, can you see what I got in the kitchen for lunch. You should find stuff for sandwiches."

I did as asked, while the mother and son duo settled at her kitchen table. The moment I realized I wanted more with Regina, I knew I'd have to figure out how to fit into her world. That I would be the one making the concessions and I was okay with it. She was worth the sacrifice. What I believed we could have together was worth it. But there was more than just her to consider. Regina wasn't the type of woman who asked permission or needed approval, yet there'd been an exchange between her and the sheriff when he'd mentioned Ms. Lucille. Almost as if he'd given her the "okay," considering he'd also lost his spouse in the accident. And as she sat with her son, I got the distinct feeling she'd need a second one from him.

I moved about, trying not to make too much noise and draw any additional attention to myself.

"What's wrong with you?" she asked.

"Nothin'."

"Boy, you were borderline rude, and you and I both know I raised you better."

Darnell and I glanced at each other at the same time. I wanted to step in and say he wasn't rude, but it wasn't my place, so I kept working on lunch.

"Sorry, Ma. I'm just not used to..." He waved his arm in my direction.

"I get that. But also, if I recall you made some comment about it being good for me or some other such nonsense. Now you want to be all up in arms."

"That was in theory. I wasn't expecting to come home and find some strange man all hugged up on you."

"First off, watch your tone. You might technically be grown, but don't let a couple hairs on your chin and a little bass in your voice get you in trouble." He opened his mouth, but she held up her hand to stop whatever he was about to say. "Secondly, what am I supposed to do. Stay single and alone forever?"

He scrubbed his hands down his face then sighed. "No. I guess seeing him was a shock is all."

She grabbed his hands, and they exchanged a quiet moment. They talked as if I wasn't in the same room, and I felt like a voyeur to their conversation.

"You're happy? He makes you happy?"

"Baby, I've always been happy. Alec being in my life is an addition not a replacement." She turned to look back at me. "But, yes, that man does make me happy. He does bring joy into my life. A different kind of joy that I was missing."

"Ew, Mom."

She whipped her head around. "Boy, hush. I'm not talking that."

I coughed to cover a laugh. Darnell glanced over at me as I plated the last sandwich and did a slight nod.

He stood, kissed his mother on the cheek, then slowly walked toward me. "That's my mom. Treat her right."

"You have my word."

He nodded slightly before giving his mom his attention again. "Gonna go check on Shonda."

Regina didn't get up until after he'd left the kitchen. "I don't know why he was doing all that posturing."

I rounded the counter and pulled her into my arms. "Because he's never seen you with anyone. You two have a bond that is clear as day. He loves you, and it makes sense he'd want to protect you." I leaned and placed a chaste kiss on her lips. "I bring you joy, huh? And I'm pretty sure *that* kind is included," I added with a wink.

She rolled her eyes, but the soft, happy expression gave away her true feelings. "Don't be lettin' that go to your head."

"Too late."

I had to admit that it would have been nice to hear her tell me those words directly, but Regina Parker was a complicated woman. And she wasn't one that seemed to get mushy or weepy. However, she cared. In her own way, she cared about me and us. I'd take it.

She placed her hands on my chest then moved to link our fingers. Regina didn't speak as she led me out the back door to the yard. It was a beautifully laid out space with pathways. Some of the flowers were dormant, but others remained alive. Lights were strung from the door and fanned out across the space ending at a pergola at the back of the yard.

"Lawrence was a good man," she spoke quietly while squeezing my hand. "His family moved to town our junior year of high school, but we didn't start dating probably until two years into college. Guess you could say it was a whirlwind after that."

She paused, and like when we were at that clearing, I didn't rush her, or speak. She kept her eyes trained on the space, staring, but not really seeing as her eyes glazed over.

"We'd only been in the house six months before he died. He and my mother-in-law had taken Darnell to Zoo Atlanta. You know that feeling you get in your gut, the one when you know something is wrong, but you just don't know exactly? The anvil in your stomach, your heart beating a tad faster than usual, and your skin tingling with hyper-awareness. I'd had that feeling that whole day."

She ran her finger beneath her eye, wiping away a tear before it had a chance to fall. Regina looked up at me. "I could have lost my son that day as well."

She took in another deep breath. Her eyes held so much sadness in the quiet unveiling she'd pushed off earlier. I wanted to siphon away her pain and grief. And I didn't want to be the cause of any more.

She squeezed my hand. "I want you to know I'm not crying over what I lost, but rather what I've found." She released a slow breath. "You're a good man, *not* Special Investigator Hodge. And you love your job. It scares the shit out of me, the thought of you being hurt...or worse, but it's what you love to do. Don't give that up for me."

"Regina..."

She held her hand up. "This isn't me saying we won't work because of it. You movin' here, changing jobs, it's a lot. And I want you to think it through. What we have is new, but I'm giving you my word that I am willing and open to doing the relationship thing. And you know I keep my word." She ended her speech with the coy smirk I was so used to seeing.

I ran my tongue along the front of my teeth, digesting everything she'd just laid out for me. She'd been open and honest. She'd let her guard down, trusted me and in what we had the potential to become. My heart pounded and my fingers tingled.

Stretching up onto her toes, Regina slid her arms around my neck, grabbed the back of my head and pressed her lips to mine. The feverish passion flamed quickly. Our mouths working with renewed hunger. I grabbed her ass, pulling her against my body, getting drunk on all she had to offer.

My dick hardened between us, forcing me to break from the kiss. "We can't keep doing this if you expect me to go back in there and have lunch with your son and his girlfriend. The 'that' he was ew-ing at is about to be really obvious in these cotton joggers."

She backed up and dropped her gaze to my crotch. "You can't scream tonight."

I licked my lips. "Neither can you."

REGINA

"THERE'S MY LADY," ALEC STATED AS SOON AS I OPENED THE door. He smiled wide as he slid his arms around my waist and leaned down to plant a soft kiss on my lips.

The nerves that had been doing ninja flips in my stomach all morning calmed a bit. We broke apart, but he kept a hold of my hand as he closed the door. We were both busy people, which had made seeing each other tricky, but laying eyes on him after two weeks, it settled on me just how much I'd missed him.

"You got here in record time," I said as we entered the kitchen.

"I may or may not have driven a little faster than the usual. Don't tell the sheriff." He winked, and I could only laugh. "Damn, baby, that looks amazing." He released my hand and headed to the island for a closer inspection of the cake.

I picked up one of the extra cupcakes. "A little treat."

The grin that started it all spread across his face. He slowly pulled the wrapper off, keeping his eyes on me. How in the hell did this man make opening a cupcake damn near naughty?

"I have my very own suga momma."

I threw my head back and laughed at his comment. That

laugh quickly died out as he moaned his appreciation of the sweet dessert while licking frosting from his thumb.

"Okay, you're keeping extra just for me, right? I'd hate to hog all these from the guest of honor." Alec finished off the remaining confection in one bite.

"Yes, greedy. Those are for you." I pointed to the other three sitting on a plate. "Hopefully, your folks enjoy them as much as you did."

He moved closer and rubbed small circles on the small of my back. "They will. And you have no idea how excited my mom and sister-in-law are to meet you."

When Alec had asked me to not only bake a cake for a baby shower but to also accompany him, I started to turn him down on the latter. It wasn't that I didn't want to meet his family, hell it only seemed fair since he'd met all of mine, but a family event like a baby shower? That had given me pause. But in the end, I'd agreed. My being present was important to him which made me want to be by his side.

I shut the lid on the box containing the vanilla and lemon cake with the light-green buttercream frosting. His brother and sister-in-law had wanted gender neutral since they had decided against finding out the sex.

"Ready?" he asked.

I nodded and gathered up the cake and cupcake boxes while Alex grabbed my suitcase and the gift bag.

He kissed my palm after we settled into his Jeep. "Thank you again. I know getting away is hard for you right now."

"I'm committed to giving our relationship a real chance. That includes making time for us. Construction is finally underway, and as my mother and niece so kindly reminded me, they could handle a day without me." I knew they meant well, but nothing stung like your family basically telling you to get lost. Even if it was for a good reason. "We're in a long-ish distance relationship, and we both have to make adjustments to make it work."

He eased out of my driveway and got us going. "Glad you feel that way."

"Why?"

The side glance he gave me had the hairs on the back of my neck standing up. It was the look of bad news incoming, and he'd waited until I was trapped in a mobile box to deliver it. When he tightened his hands on the steering wheel, my nerves stormed back full force.

"I got a job offer. Possibly."

"Why do you sound so unsure about it?"

He blew out a breath. "Well, I got an assignment. I'll be taking over for one of the Atlanta investigators while she's on maternity leave."

I shifted in my seat. There was something he wasn't saying. "This is a good thing, right? You're being recognized for your work. And it gets you back to the city."

"That's the thing. It could keep me in the city." He shot another quick glance in my direction and his statement sank in. "According to my chief, she's thinking of staying at home, and I'm on the short list to replace her."

I pressed my lips together and took in a slow breath. "Congratulations. You've talked about how small-town living isn't for you. This is a big deal."

"Yeah, but that was before." He glanced at me again with a half-smile.

I twisted so my back was pressed against the door. I was of two minds. On one hand, I wanted him to follow his dreams. He enjoyed his career and wanted back in the city. On the other, trying to see each other had been tricky when we were less than an hour away from each other. Four...

"Either way, this is good news, and I'm proud of you for making the short list. It says a lot about how much your coworkers and boss respect you." His smile grew, and I reached over to grab his hand. "When will you find out for sure?"

He shrugged. "I have to report next week but... I don't know. I'm concerned about the distance for us."

"It's four hours, not like you're moving out of state. Plus, I have my fancy food truck. Tricia has already been researching festivals. If you want this, you should absolutely accept it."

"You really think so?" He squeezed his fingers around mine and took in a breath. "Nothing is a done deal."

I drew small circles in his palm with my thumb. "Do you want the position?"

He lifted a shoulder. "If you'd asked me a few months ago I would have said yes in a heartbeat. Now..."

It was a romantic ideal. Chivalrous almost. The thought of him wanting to change his life around for me; it hit me right in the heart and warmed me throughout. He was serious and dedicated, but he had his own career and aspirations. And I wasn't sure I wanted to shoulder the guilt of him passing up on them for something that was still so new, even if a small part of me hoped he would.

"Alec, this is what you want for your job. Your career. I told you before when you were talking about the position in Madison, don't make your decisions because of me. If you want this job, I promise you, I'm willing to make it work."

"Okay, I see what you're saying. And whether it's this or taking over for Chief Morris, you won't be the deciding factor. But I won't lie and say you won't be a consideration."

"That's fair."

The rest of the trip was uneventful, which was good because my mind continued to swirl with the information about his job. As we entered into a well-manicured subdivision, my previous reservations returned. It'd been a long time since I'd had to do the meet the parents thing. To do so at a family and friends event like a baby shower somehow added extra pressure, but also lessened it at the same time because the focus wouldn't solely be on me.

"Hey, you're not worried, are you?"

I shook my head. "Nope. Time for me to make your family love me as much as mine apparently loves you.

He winked. "What can I say, I'm a lovable guy."

I rolled my eyes and huffed a quiet laugh. We pulled into the driveway of a two-story brick home that reminded me of the *Home Alone* house, but smaller.

"Your parents have a beautiful home."

He leaned forward to peer out the windshield. "Not the mini subdivision your family has, but it's home." He placed two fingers on my chin and turned me to face him before leaning in for a quick kiss. "Thank you again."

"Will you stop thanking me. I want to be here with you." I linked my fingers with his. "You've been in my world, it's time for me to be in yours."

He rolled his tongue along his bottom lip, and with a final squeeze to my hand, he turned to exit the Jeep. I grabbed the gift bag while he carried the cake boxes. Before we could ring the bell, the door flew open, and a tall, slender woman squealed, "Finally."

Alec juggled the boxes to accommodate the hug she moved in for. The distinct lack of a protruding belly told me this woman was not the sister-in-law.

"Le-Le. No one told me you'd be here."

"Eh, I wasn't sure I'd make it, but my case wrapped up and there was no way I was missing this." She straightened and set her sights on me. Her eyes went wide, and she clapped her hands together. "And you must be Regina." I had no chance to reply before I was engulfed in a hug. "I'm so excited." She linked her arm through mine and tugged me into the house.

I glanced back over my shoulder at Alec who mouthed an, "I'm sorry," as I was speed-walked through the foyer to a large, formal living room. The space was tastefully decorated with streamers and balloons. A club chair sat off from the rest with an arch of balloons over it. Sitting in a dining chair next to the makeshift throne was a man I immediately knew to be Alec's brother. Knowing Alec had a twin was one thing; seeing him live and in person was another, and my eyes went to him first. Unlike Alec, this version was clean shaven, otherwise, they were an exact replica.

"She's here," my enthusiastic companion announced. "A little introduction since my brother can't be bothered."

"You haven't given me a chance," he bellowed as he walked by.

She rolled her eyes. "Anyway. I'm the favorite, also known as Leila." Alec's brother mumbled something under his breath, and she pointed at him. "That one is Thing 2, also known as Terrance. My fiancée, Megan." She indicated at a dark-skinned woman with an impressive curly fro.

"Favorite my ass," Alec commented as he walked back in, arms free. He slid a hand onto my lower back. A simple act, but a clear message and one I fully leaned into.

As the older woman stood from the couch, Alec stepped forward, then bent so she could kiss his cheek.

"Hey, Mom. Regina, this is my mother, Delores, and my father, William."

"Forgive my daughter. She's been waiting a long time for this moment," she said, turning to face me. "We all have. We're happy to meet you, Regina."

"Nice to meet you all as well." I shook her outstretched hand. It was her eyes. Large, round, and so dark they almost seemed black. He had his mother's eyes. And, in comparison to my own mother, her welcome was much more subdued.

A loud, "Uncle Alec!" Followed by the pounding of feet. I turned to see a blur of pink and glitter. Alec kneeled, arms wide, in time to catch the little girl, who launched herself at him. Hearing him talk about his niece was one thing, but being witness to the overflowing love from each of them was a different level.

Alec's father quietly took the gift bags from me as the sister-in-law introduced herself. "Thank you for coming. And for making a cake. Alec...well, he's been singing your praises for a while now."

I twisted my lips into a smile when I glanced at him. His niece had attached herself to his back and was calling for him to give her a ride, which he obliged. She had him wrapped around her finger, and it was adorable.

"You're welcome. And congratulations."

She placed one hand on her large stomach and the other on her back. "Thank you. I'm so ready to be done."

"I can imagine. I knew how I was toward the end of my pregnancy."

"Alec didn't mention you had children," Delores said. There was an exchange of looks, and I understood what Alec had meant when he'd pointed out the same sort of thing back in Madison.

"Just the one. He's twenty. A sophomore at Morehouse."

More silent communication and the worry from earlier crept back in. I was unsure of what issue she had, the fact that I had a child, or his age. Either way, I was ready on the defense for whatever comment might come, but none did.

"That's a good school," William remarked. "The boys had thought about going there."

"Janet, cake's in the kitchen. You need to go check it out," Alec called while running around the room to the sound of his niece's joyful laughs.

The group all filed out of the living room, and I followed suit, moving deeper into the Hodge home. It was beautifully decorated. I stopped to admire the wall of photos in the hall. This was real.

"In awe, aren't you?" Alec whispered.

I glanced over my shoulder, his niece was barreling toward her father. "Excuse me?"

"That I was always this good-looking. My brother had to grow into it, but me...sexy from the get."

I snorted a laugh. "Cocky from the get as well?"

He shrugged and slipped his hand into mine. When we entered the kitchen, Janet and Delores were putting the cupcakes on a silver tiered stand while Terrance was taking pictures of the cake.

"This is beautiful. And if it tastes half as good as it looks, I'll have to actually say that Imitation Me was right for a change."

"Thirty-two years, and you still haven't gotten it through your head, I'm the original. You're the bad copy."

They bickered back and forth, and I took it all in. I already knew he was a good man, but witnessing him with his family, despite some of my earlier reservations, my choice to commit to a relationship with Alec was solidified.

❧

As we got ready for bed, I quietly watched him while I twisted my hair up before securing it under my scarf. "You didn't tell your parents I had a kid?"

He stripped down to his boxers and shrugged. "Didn't see it as a big deal. Why?"

The rest of the day had gone pretty well. I hadn't gotten any additional odd vibes from his mother, but the awkward interaction at the first meeting had stuck in the back of my mind.

"I don't know, she just seemed surprised, and it looked like you two were having that secret communication you accused me of."

He walked over to where I stood next to the bed and pulled me into a hug. "That was more about me most likely. I went from never wanting to be in a serious relationship or have kids, to dating and basically having a ready-made family." Alec leaned and kissed me softly. "I promise, you were a hit. I don't know how you missed the 'I told you so' smirks my mom gave me all night."

His answer made sense and I had noticed a couple of the smiles and nods in his direction. So, I chalked up all the possible negative connotations to how I'd feel if Darnell brought home a woman ten years his senior. I could have been projecting because at the end of the day his family was friendly and welcoming, and I'd had a great time.

His other statement danced in my head. "A ready-made family" ...those words rolled off his tongue easily and without hesitation. Yes, Darnell was grown, but we were a package deal, and how easily Alec accepted that fact... I wrapped my arms around his neck, pressing my lips to his in a slow act of appreciation. He ran his hands down my sides and began gathering up my gown and his dick hardened against my stomach.

I pulled back and stared at him. "What do you think you're doing?"

A sexy, lopsided grin appeared. "You know exactly what I'm doing."

"Are you out of your mind? I'm not having sex with you in your parents' house," I whispered.

"Why not?"

I untangled myself from his arms and frowned at him. "Because it's your parents' house that's why."

He hugged me from behind. "That's what makes it exciting. It's one of those teenage fantasy things I never got to live out."

I laughed and shook my head. "You're serious? That was your teenage fantasy? Having sex while your parents slept down the hall?"

He slid his hands up to cup my breasts, rolling my nipples between his fingers. He lowered his voice, and the hairs of his beard brushed against my cheek. "Yeah, but those fantasies usually involved me with a model or two."

I leaned back into him, enjoying his hypnotic teasing. "Why does that not surprise me?"

"I'm not a complicated man," he murmured against my ear.

I spun in his arms and reached between our bodies to stroke him. "Just a horny one."

He sank his teeth into his bottom lip and groaned. The

primal sound doused my last bit of reservation. This man had appeared in my life at one of my lowest points and done all he could to make it not as terrible without expecting anything in return. The gravity and importance of that would never be forgotten.

I kept my eyes on his as I moved my hand up and down his length, squeezing when I got to the head and down again. His mouth hung open and he placed his warm palm over mine to aid in my movements.

I kissed his chest. "Is this how that fantasy of yours went?"

"Mm-hm, only this is better."

I planted more kisses along his chest, stretching up to place one at the base of his neck. "How's that?"

He looked down at me and released another low moan as I continued to stroke him. "Because it's you."

His answer made me pause as I gazed into his dark, sincere eyes. My heart stuttered and I pulled in a shaky breath, tingling from head to toe. "On the bed." Emotions and lust made my voice scratchy.

He didn't ask why, instead he yanked down his underwear on the way before settling, legs wide, and grinning too broadly. His beautiful cock stood erect and ready for action. I walked my fingers up his leg, stopping just inside his inner thigh. He wanted a fantasy? I'd give him one.

Climbing onto the bed, I settled between his legs and grasped his large dick in my hands. The skin, velvety smooth and warm beneath my grip. I licked my lips in anticipation of the treat that awaited me. Up, down, with a slight twist, Alec watched my movements. His breath hitched when I leaned forward and pressed a kiss to the head before swirling my tongue around the tip, sliding it through the tiny slit. A trickle of precum, salty on my taste buds.

I licked and caressed his length. The tease was part of the fun for me. I took power in the seduction, letting my mouth make love to his cock. Keeping my eyes on him, I wrapped my lips around his stiffness and slowly lowered down. He whimpered low and the sound electrified me, driving my own desire higher. As I swallowed more of him, I wanted to make his toes curl and obliterate his senses. And I knew I could.

My nipples tightened as the head of his dick rubbed against the roof of my mouth, creating a sensual tickling sensation. I inhaled deep, hints of citrus and expensive tobacco swirled around my nose, getting me high on the essence of Alec. I cupped his balls, gently massaging them, and bobbled my head up and down along his dick, taking him deeper each time. My pussy throbbed with arousal. I relaxed my throat and he slipped down further. When I hummed, he gripped the sheets and tossed his head from side to side.

Pulling up, I licked my lips and stroked him while watching the rapid rise and fall of his chest. Our eyes met and his signature grin made its appearance. The sight of it, *of him*, sent my heart into overdrive. Taking in a breath, I returned his smile before taking him deep into my mouth once again. He filled me in more ways than one.

I slipped my other hand lower beneath his balls, applying gentle pressure. He grabbed a pillow and held it over his face, but his muffled cries still rang in my ears. He was falling apart, and I wanted to be the final tug to undo the thread. I moved faster, the in and out of his dick added to my own arousal. My nipples were hard, and my pussy tingled.

Alec's stomach clenched, his legs locked, and his body jolted as he lost all control, shooting his release down my throat while he screamed out from behind the pillow. His intense and unrestrained reaction coaxed my body through its own gentle orgasm, but I kept sucking through the shudders until he started begging.

"Regina...baby...wait...whew...just..." Alec's legs drooped to the side.

He was spent; chest rising and falling quickly, mouth hanging open, and forearm slung across his face. And I mentally patted myself on the back from achieving my goal. As I kissed my way up his body, my head swam, and a tantalizing current danced throughout me. I was drunk on life, lust... *love*. I took in a calming breath when I settled beside him. He stared at the ceiling, looking a bit dazed, but felt around until he clasped my hand.

"I am...that was...When I saw you with the crawfish, I knew my soul would leave my body and I was not wrong." He turned to look at me, a lazy smile on his handsome face.

I laughed at his statement, then leaned forward to press a soft kiss to his lips. "Fantasy fulfilled?"

He nodded. "From day fucking one." He softly pressed his mouth to mine again. "Love you, Ms. Parker."

I ran my thumb across his lips. Warmth bloomed through me as I stared deep into his dark brown eyes. Sweet, and sincere. The words sat at the tip of my tongue, three little ones I hadn't uttered, at least not for this meaning of them.

I inched closer to him, and with my heart full, the last holdout disintegrated. "I love you as well, Special Investigator."

He claimed my lips and I let myself get lost in the affection, in the comfort, and in the security of being in love.

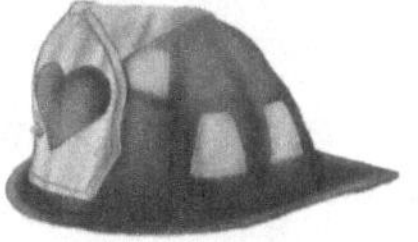

REGINA

CONSTANT NOISE HAD NEVER BEEN SO WELCOMED. BANGING, whirling, sawing, shouts, all of it enough to give me a headache, but I enjoyed the hell out of it. The loudness meant progress. The loudness meant things were on their way back to normal. Or a new normal. With a line of eager customers, I didn't have time to let my mind wander back to my day with Alec's family. Even if my time spent in my food truck had me thinking of him. And missing him.

We'd talked on the phone nearly every day. And his sneaky ass had coaxed me into phone sex more times than I cared to admit. Though to be fair, it wasn't like he had to work that hard, but he'd had me feeling like we were doing something naughty and a little illicit all the same. Just like the night at his parents' house. It made for a good time, and a decent stand-in, but nothing beat the real deal.

Doc Johnson's approach forced me to put my wanton thoughts back in a box and focus on work. "Mornin', Doc. Large black coffee and an apple turnover coming right up."

"Thanks, Regina." He peered in, then scrunched his brow. "Where's ya momma today?"

Cassie set his pastry on the ledge next to the full cup while I rang up his order. "These new working conditions have made her live more of the retired life. But she'll be back to stressin' me out once we reopen."

The space was only so big, two people max with all the equipment, so that meant me and one employee most of the time. I felt terrible that their hours were cut, so I tried to have them rotate as much as possible, which meant Momma got side-lined more times than not.

He slid his credit card back into his wallet. "I wish I could be living the retired life, but your friend doesn't want to cooperate. She needs to be more like you, the good daughter and carrying on the family business."

"Now, Doc Johnson, you got that new fella." Doctor Michaels wasn't exactly new; he'd moved to town ten years ago and split his time between the hospital and seeing patients at Doc Johnson's office.

He waved me off with a grunt. "Nothing against Dr. Michaels, but it's called *Johnson* Family Medicine. It ain't right I have to leave a practice I built to someone that's not a Johnson."

There'd been times I wondered if Irene had really wanted to be a doctor or if she simply stepped in where her brother had failed. Poor Evan knew medicine was not for him after he passed out at the thought of dissecting a frog. Instead, he'd gone the legal route and had a successful small law office in Savannah. He'd helped me sort out everything after Lawrence's death.

I leaned forward and rested my arms on the ledge while Cassie continued to take orders. "I understand. I do. But it's not that easy. There ain't much in the way of investment banking 'round here. What's Derrick supposed to do? Be a teller over at Madison Community Bank?"

After Cynthia's return, the thought had danced in the back of my mind. How great it would be to have us all together in town again. Sure, Irene visited, more than Cynthia had, but still, it was hard to have her gone. Though I never voiced that to either of them. They'd had their lives to live, and I'd had mine.

We'd maintained via weekly virtual girls' nights and annual trips. I shared part of Doc Johnson's desire to have Irene home, but I'd never tell him. He didn't need any more fuel for his guilt-trip fire.

He grunted again, but a slight wry grin formed. "Guess I need to get out the way so you can work. Tell your folks I said hi. And that daddy of yours is past due for his checkup."

I pushed to standing and stretched out my back as best I could. "Momma will have him there next week."

The rest of the morning flew by. After cleaning up the truck, I locked up then headed inside the bakery. Music blasted from a radio in the corner, I don't know how they heard what was playing over the tools and yelling. All traces of the fire had been stripped out. The usual scents of sugar and coffee had been replaced with sawdust mixed with an earthy mud undertone. Not the best, but miles above the charred soot aroma that had been seared into me since the night of the fire.

I carefully weaved my way through in search of the man in charge. I found Marcel in the lobby with MJ, having a conversation. They were looking at the plans for the building, and I only caught bits of what they said as I approached. Both men smiled when they saw me.

MJ gave me a quick hug. "It's coming together, Ms. Regina. Dad and I were just discussing the possibility of leaving some of the brick exposed."

With the drywall down, the original walls of the old building stood in all their glory, bare for the world to see. I'd honestly forgotten that the brick was even there.

"The front wall by the door is in pretty bad shape so we'd probably want to simply rebuild with new studs and re-sheet that one, but the other three are looking good. I could get my mason in to sure up any loose ones, but it could give the place a new look," Marcel added.

I tapped my chin as early memories came back to me. "I actually think it would be going back to the original. If memory serves, the drywall was put up during the time Grams was in charge. She'd wanted something more polished."

A soft smile tugged at my lips as the scattered memories solidified. Nothing much had been changed until I'd done minor updates five years prior.

"Three exposed, one drywalled?" MJ asked.

I shook my head. "I'm liking the idea of just the back wall behind the counter. Gives it more of a focus to me."

They both nodded. "We can make that happen," Marcel said. MJ excused himself leaving his father to walk me toward the exit. "Cyn told me they finally tracked down the bastard."

I nodded. Trent had been located hiding out in Miami. His parents were instrumental in tracking him down with their house on the line. "Yup. Pops said they were coordinating with Miami PD to get him transferred to the county jail, where he'll stay until the trial about the theft."

I massaged my temples. I couldn't process all the information Pops had said about the investigation and having to still prove Trent had set the fire. So, he may have been located, but nothing was a done deal. The tension crawled up my neck, pooled at the base, then seemingly shot out like hot arrows ping-ponging around my head.

Marcel wrapped his arm around my shoulders. "It'll all work out. And we're all here for you."

"Thanks, Marcel. I should get out of the way and let you work."

He followed me out, walking me around the side of the building to the back parking lot. I hit the unlock button for my car. It had been months, but I still wasn't used to my day ending so damn early.

"Are you keeping my wife all night?"

I climbed in and cranked the engine to get the heat started. "I'll try not to, but make no promises."

He laughed then shut my door. With everything with the

bakery on top of Alec, I found myself in desperate need of some time with my ladies.

⚜

MY PHONE DINGED JUST as Cynthia entered my kitchen through the side door with pizza in hand.

"Irene is bailing on us tonight," I said as way of greeting.

She slid the large box onto the island, then pulled her phone from her back pocket. "Damn, is that the message? I heard my phone go off but hadn't checked yet."

I lifted the lid and inhaled the deliciousness that was Vito's. My stomach growled in response.

Cynthia sighed and put the device away. "Guess we can't be mad at the doctor being needed for a late appointment."

"S'pose not, but she doesn't normally work evenings, so hopefully whatever it is isn't too big of an emergency." I placed two slices onto my plate and carried it over to the table.

Cynthia poured herself a glass of Chardonnay after she'd joined me. "So..." She let the word hang as she bit into her meal.

"So what?"

"Have you told him you want him to take the job in Madison?"

I took a gulp of wine to buy time. When I'd told her about Alec's job options, never once did I say I wanted him here. But I should have known she'd read between the lines. "I don't want him to take the chief position. I want him to take the job that makes him happiest. Which is what I told him and you."

"Regina, that man is in love with you. You said he told you as much when you let him stay here. There is no harm in letting him know you feel the same."

I pressed my lips together and straightened in my chair. "That ship has sailed."

"What? Oh my god, seriously? The great Regina Parker done

finally fell for another man."

"Whatever, heffa."

I narrowed my eyes at her, and she responded by swaying side to side while chewing on her pizza. I ignored her "I knew it" dance and finished off my own slice.

"Regardless, I'm not sure I'm adjusting well. I miss him. Yeah, we talk, video chat, but I don't know, I'd like to see him, see him. You know? And I'm not sure how I feel about needing him. About wanting him to be around as much as I do."

"Why is that a bad thing?"

I sighed. "For a lot of reasons. It's not a dependency thing...I don't know how to explain it, but a little part of me is terrified. Plus, his job..." I couldn't fully understand it myself. I'd never been the clingy, needy type. I wanted him to live his life, have his interests, do what he loved as much as I had those things, but I also had this unexplained urge to lay eyes on him more often than I'd currently been able to.

Her face softened. "I get it. When it's been just you for the most part, giving your heart...it's a leap of faith into unknown waters no matter what." She paused and smiled at me. "As for his job, he's trying to change it. Take on something less dangerous. Look, I'm not a believer in everything happens for a reason. Because, honestly, what could possibly be the reason for some shitty things?" She reached across to grab my hand, giving it a squeeze. "But what I do know is this man has come into your life when he was apparently needed. This might be the right time for you. Speak your truth, and let it happen. Because from where I'm sitting, he seems to be all in with you."

She wasn't wrong. I knew she wasn't wrong. The fact that I was the only woman he'd apparently ever taken to meet his family proved she wasn't wrong. In an ideal world, I would be thrilled to have Alec in town, or at least closer than hours away. But despite what my friend believed, and my own conflicting emotions on the situation, I stood by my choice of telling him to take the position he wanted most.

ALEC

A MONTH. THAT'S HOW LONG IT'D BEEN SINCE I'D SEEN
Regina. On one hand, I was thrilled to be working more as an
investigator. Though being back in the city didn't hold the same
appeal I'd thought it would. Yes, doing investigations meant I
was off the truck and doing the safer job, which made both
Regina and my mother happy. But making Regina happy meant
little to nothing as the new, safer job kept us apart.

The grand opening was closing in, so she was tied up. I'd
promised her I'd be there, and come hell or high water, I would
not miss her big day.

While I figured it out, some much-needed decompression
time was in order. I wasn't sure what was worse—sleeping at the
bunk house or being over thirty and living with your parents
again, even if it was temporarily. Slowly, I made my way through
the semi-crowded bar and in search of my friend and ex-
coworker Reggie. We'd worked together for seven years before
I'd gotten the investigator job and moved. He was the one guy I
kept in touch with the most. Probably because of the guys, we
were the only two not married or in a serious long-term relationship. We'd partied and hit up all the hot spots whenever we'd had
a weekend off at the same time.

I spotted him sitting at a high top, flirting with the waitress.

"Hey, man, how's it going?"

"Not bad, not bad," I replied. "Have you been waiting long?"

"Nah. I just got here not long ago myself. Tina here was just getting my order."

There'd been a time when the tall, curvy woman who was all legs in her short shorts would have had me turning on the charm and getting into a friendly competition with Reggie to see who could get her number, if not more, first. But as I smiled while shrugging out of my coat, a general, polite greeting was all I was inclined to offer.

After she took our order and left, Reggie kept his eyes glued to her ass before he leaned forward. "What was up with that?"

"With what?"

"You barely glanced at our waitress. I know it's been a while, but if I remember correctly, she's right up your alley."

I picked up the menu and glanced over the food options. "I'm seeing someone."

"Shit, man...I'm seeing a few someones myself."

I laughed and shook my head. "Yeah, well mine is not in the plural."

His eyes went wide, and he jerked back in his chair. "Wha... You shittin' me. Mr. Bachelor-For-Life got so bored down in Savannah some woman managed to rope you in. Whatcha you do, knock her up?"

Tina returned and handed us our drinks, we both thanked her, and I put in our food orders. I swirled the ice around in the glass before taking a sip of my Jack and Coke. "Man, please. I may have me a steady lady, but still no juniors, and I plan on keeping it that way. My brother keeps me supplied with all the littles I can handle."

"So, then boredom. We need to get you out of that place and back to the action. The clubs, the after spots, and all the variety of the fairer sex. I knew you taking your ass down there would fuck with your head."

"Believe me, man, if you met Regina, you'd know boredom wouldn't even be in your vocabulary."

Reggie was about four years younger than me, so I couldn't entirely fault his reaction. Hell, a few months ago I probably would have reacted the same way. But now... My mother would be fucking ecstatic to find out she was right. Which made the new choices I had to make that much more complicated.

❧

I PULLED into the driveway at my parents' house.

Dad was rounding the corner just as I stepped in. "Hey, son." He spun out of the way at the sound of pounding feet. Mia ran full force toward me, wrapped her arms around my neck, and squeezed with more strength than a four-year-old should possess after I scooped her up.

"Shouldn't you be sleeping?"

She shook her head, her beaded hair clicking with the action. "Granpy said I could wait up for you."

"He did, huh? You know, I never got to stay up past my bedtime."

"Probably because you were bad," she fired back without a beat.

"Being granddad instead of dad gives me way more leeway."

I transferred Mia to my back and headed toward the family room, where my mom was putting away the dolls.

"Hey, Ma." I kissed her cheek then deposited my passenger onto the sofa.

"Hey, baby. How was your friend?"

"Good. Bummed I called it an early night. But I had a special little lady to see." I tickled my niece, who erupted into a fit of giggles.

Mom swatted my arm. "Stop. You're getting her all riled up before bed. It's bad enough I had to stop that one from sneaking her sweets." She thumbed toward my dad, who held his hands up in mock innocence.

Dad settled into his recliner. "You look troubled, son."

I took a seat on the sectional with Mia plopping herself in my lap to watch the cartoons Mom put on the TV. It wasn't missed on me that neither of them seemed to be in a hurry to follow the schedule my sister-in-law set. But that's what grandparents were for.

Mom sat beside me and tapped my leg. "What's going on, Alec?"

I shook my head. "You can take the worry out of your voice. It's nothing bad. Just work...mostly."

Dad's thick brows drew together. "I thought things were going well. You were doing more investigations, which made your mother happy, no running into burning buildings. And I thought you said your supervisors were impressed with you."

I squeezed my mom's hand. I knew she worried, as mothers do. And girlfriends, apparently. "Yes. That's all going well."

"But?" Mom prompted.

I shifted Mia to the cushion beside me, then sat up. "But I have the opportunity I thought I wanted, but now I'm not so sure."

Dad tilted his head. "Why not?"

Mia kicked me, and I turned to see she'd fallen asleep just that quickly. "I'll carry her to bed."

"She'll be fine for a bit. Tell us what's going on," Mom pushed.

"Mom, you'll be happy to know you were right."

She laughed. "I usually am. But about what exactly?"

"About knowing the one when you least expect it." She and Dad exchanged surprised expressions before Mom pretended to faint from the shock. I rolled my eyes and laughed softly at her antics. "Anyway, Regina. I have two opportunities: one that takes me closer to her and one that, well, keeps me here."

Dad propped his feet up. "Ah, yes. Madison Island, right? Her friend runs the B&B we were going to stay at until Janet had that scare."

I nodded remembering the frantic call my mom had made saying Janet was being rushed to the hospital and they were on Mia duty. After that, they canceled all plans on leaving the city so they'd be close just in case something else had happened, which thankfully hadn't been the case.

Mom squeezed my arm. "Have you talked to her about it?"

I rubbed my hands together and swallowed the lump in my throat. "I have. And, well, she thinks I should be where I'm happiest."

Mom smiled. "Son, Regina is a reasonable, level-headed woman. We enjoyed getting to meet her and we're thrilled you've found that special someone." She paused and I knew the "but" part of her statement was incoming. "When you took the position in Savannah, you'd said it would be temporary. A stepping-stone to getting back to the city."

"It was. But now, with me actually being in a relationship, it seems counterproductive to commit then move away."

"Well, son," Dad started. "It's a couple hours' drive. If you want this, and the new relationship with Regina, you'll figure out how to make it work. She seems to be supportive of whatever decision you make. I get it's hard, but if it's meant to be, it'll be."

Make it work. I blew out a breath and rested back against the couch. It'd been a month since I'd actually laid eyes on Regina outside of video calls. How in the hell would we juggle more distance? She'd wanted me to follow my dreams and do what I loved, and the city position had been my endgame.

As I got settled in bed for the night, my mind went back to the conversation with my parents. I still had time before I had to make a decision, but not too much. Reaching over to the nightstand, I grabbed my phone and dialed Regina's number.

"Evenin', Special Investigator."

I smiled at the continued use of that moniker. "Evenin' your-self Ms. Parker. How was your day?"

"Same old, same old. Busy day on the truck. Did some inventory and placed orders. Got updates from Marcel on the progress. How was yours?"

Mention of progress made me feel good, it helped undercut the anger and frustration that she'd been put in the predicament to begin with. The pictures she'd been sending showed the bakery was coming along well and I couldn't wait to see it in person.

"Mine was good. Wrapped up the warehouse fire investigation. Looks like the owner was involved. And I had drinks with an old friend. It was good to get out and catch up."

"You're really enjoying your time back in the city?"

"Yeah, other than living with my parents. Though I do have excellent memories associated with the room now." I laughed when she groaned and could almost picture her rolling her eyes at my comment.

"Anyway. Have you started looking for a place?"

I sat up at her question. "No. I haven't made a decision about the position yet. I'm still considering my options. Why are you packing my bags already?"

She let out a long sigh. "There you go taking stuff all personal again. It's not like that. I told you I'm committed to this relationship thing. That includes if you happen to be farther away because you got an amazing opportunity."

"Yeah, I know. It is. I won't lie, it's been great, and I've learned a lot more."

"Well, see. You're enjoying the work and being back in Atlanta. Would I love to see you more? Of course, I have no issue admitting that, but what I want more is for you to be happy with your job. And where you live."

"Why, Ms. Parker did you just admit to missing me."

Another huffed sigh, but I was sure she had a smile on her face. "I don't know why I bother with your foolish ass."

"You know why."

"I'm gonna hang up on you."

The playful bickering was who we were, and I would probably never tire of the back and forth because underneath the truth came out. I massaged my temple. The city was in my blood. I was handling bigger, more complex cases. Taking the Atlanta assignment would be a major step for my career. And we could make it work, just like my dad said. Just like she'd said. She was committed to the relationship. But did *I* want to do a long-distance thing? That was the million-dollar question.

REGINA

AFTER SEVEN LONG MONTHS, THE DAY WAS FINALLY HERE. JUST a Bit of Sugar would be open for business. The food truck was great and all, and we had plans to keep it, with Tricia already registering us for a few upcoming festivals, but I'd missed my shop. I'd missed the hustle and bustle. I'd missed the conversations with my customers and having them sit and enjoy the space and atmosphere.

Finally, the weight that had been on my chest since the night of the fire had lifted. I was back! And surrounded by the people who meant the most to me. Irene had flown in for the weekend. My son was here. My siblings. Everyone. *Mostly...*

Full staff was on deck for the day. They were just as excited about the opening. My sister and brother-in-law were getting last minute instructions from Tricia. I could tell she took great pleasure in bossing her parents around. Darnell and Shonda were helping Nick load the last of the items into the display case. A small crowd had gathered outside, awaiting the ceremonial ribbon cutting.

"That Marcel Lewis sho out did himself," Momma said, coming to stand beside me.

I slipped my arm around her waist and squeezed. "He did. We're back and will be better than ever."

She twisted her head to look at me, a soft approving smile on her face. "With you in charge, I have no doubt. I told you everything would work out."

The place was better than I'd expected. It was the same, yet somehow so much more. The soft green on the walls with our logo emblazoned in the middle of the windowless one. Hanging around it were family photos. My great grandmother on our first ever opening day. My grandmother, my mother...the women who have all nurtured this business. Myself included standing proud with my mother the day she handed me the reins. Us in front of the food truck. A wall of history, and it was the most beautiful thing in the world.

The new cases were filled with all the delights we'd had to cut out with the limited menu. The exposed brick wall housed the new menu board, bright and colorful just as it had always been. Sugar and coffee in the air. I inhaled deep. Damn, I'd missed that smell. The bistro tables outside were ready, as were the ones inside. The cozy seating nook with comfy chairs and side tables was inviting, and hopefully would encourage people to stay even longer.

My heart was full. My family was here, as were my friends. I glanced at Cynthia and Irene through the large front window. It was time.

And he wasn't here.

Six weeks since we'd last seen each other. He'd been in high demand, but he'd assured me come hell or high water he'd be here today. And yet...

Momma squeezed my hand. "You ready?"

"Hell yes!" I motioned for Tricia and blinked rapidly at the figure strolling through the double steel doors, sliding a pink apron over his head. The same apron I'd given him the day he'd shown up to work and he'd never returned it. *Alec had made it.* My heart skipped a beat. The disappointment in him missing my big day dissipated, and an eerily happy calm eased over me.

"Now you're ready," Momma whispered and winked.

Together me, Momma, and Tricia walked to the front door. I took a breath and reveled in the glorious soft click of the lock turning. The moment we pulled it open, and the bell chimed, applause erupted from the crowd.

Flanked on either side by my mom and niece, I snipped the green ribbon taped across the door. "Folks, we are once again open for business."

More cheers and claps. Hollers of congratulations. Each bit ping-ponged through me, warming me from the inside out and causing a burning behind my eyes as I tried not to cry. We stepped to the side and let them file in. Mayor Harrison hugged me and talked about how excited she was that we were back.

This was my home. My community. And I was once again whole. Last to enter were Cynthia and Irene. They squealed as they got closer, and we embraced in a tight group hug with Momma and Tricia joining in. Momma broke free to give some attention to Marcel and apparently hung on too long because Dad's voice boomed from behind us.

"Watch yourself there, Lewis."

"Oh, hush, you cranky old man," Momma shot back but strolled to him, planting a big kiss on him.

Tricia was called to the counter, and I was left with my girls.

"It looks amazing," Irene commented, squeezing my hand for a moment before letting it go. "You'd never know that... Well, that's behind us now."

My response was cut off by Alec's approach. "Can I get one of those?"

I crossed my arms and looked up at him. "One of what?"

The grin that started it all appeared. Instead of answering, he engulfed me in his arms, and I instantly melted against him. I hadn't wanted to acknowledge how much I'd wanted him here until the moment he was back and in the flesh.

I pulled away. "You were late."

"I missed you, too."

Irene cleared her throat beside me.

"Oh, sorry. Alec, I'd like you to meet Irene."

Alec extended his hand. "Ah, the third Musketeer. Nice to finally meet you."

She looked him up and down with a smirk. "You too."

I rolled my eyes. "Stop actin' up."

"What I do? I am being polite to your *boy*friend." The way she sang out the word was followed up with laughs from her and Cynthia, and Alec had the nerve as well.

"Y'all not g'on get on my nerves today."

Cynthia and Marcel both greeted Alec before they pulled Irene away. There was activity all around us, but as we stood facing each other it all faded away.

"It looks better in person."

"You still stalking me on social media?"

"I call it being supportive." He winked and my heart did another flip.

I smacked my lips. "I suppose."

He placed his fingers on my chin, tilting my head up for a quick kiss. "I have really missed you," he whispered.

I smiled against his lips. "Me too."

"This has been a long day coming."

I linked my fingers with his. "True. But...thank you for being here. It means a lot to me."

He squeezed our joined hands. "I told you I wouldn't miss it."

The calm associated with Alec settled over me. From the beginning, he'd had an interest. The way he'd cared about my business, about me. A horrible event brought us together, but damn if I hadn't come out on the other side with a hell of a lot more than I'd bargained for. His presence warmed me. Settled me. And the distance we'd had between us had bothered me more than I'd wanted him to know. But him being beside me now, I knew I wanted to share everything and nothing with him. I wanted him here.

The door chimed, and Chief Morris strolled in. "Regina!" He held his arms out wide, and I moved forward to hug him. "I knew you'd be back. Nothing can keep a good woman down."

"Thanks, Chief."

He made a tsking sound. "Not for much longer." He looked over to Alec. "Morning, Chief Hodge."

My eyes went wide as I shifted my attention between the two men. Alec lowered his head, and Chief Morris seemed to realize he'd let the proverbial cat out of the bag and quickly excused himself. Alec opened his mouth to speak, but I shook my head to cut him off. I grabbed his hand and pulled him through the lobby to the back, ignoring the curious stares of my friends and family.

"Say what now?" I asked only after we were behind the privacy of my closed office door.

"I was going to tell you."

"When? We talk on the phone most nights. You never bothered to mention you took the job here."

"I know. I wanted to tell you in person. And after all of this. This is your moment to shine." He tilted his head. "Why do you seem pissed at the news?"

I began pacing. "I'm not...just..." I stopped and met his gaze head on.

When we'd talked, sure, he'd mentioned missing me, but also went on and on about how it was good to be back in the city. Hitting up his old stomping grounds, favorite restaurants, spending more time with his niece and new nephew.

"I honestly am shocked, Special Investigator Hodge. The position in Atlanta, it was everything you wanted."

He stepped closer and rested his hands on my hips. "It was everything I thought I wanted. And I know, you again told me to take the job that would make me happy, and we'd work the other stuff out. That's what I did. So, it's Chief Hodge, with a little special investigating on the side. I can keep the area I'd handled from Savannah and take over the Madison station."

I frowned. "You don't like small-town life. Are you going to be satisfied here?"

"With you, I'm always satisfied."

"Thank you. I...I wanted you here, but I didn't want to say and be the reason you gave up a career move you'd been after."

"I know, because you love me." He grinned so wide when he spoke those words I thought his face might actually split in two. "And I love you. I weighed all my options and here is where I want to be, no doubt about it."

My heart raced with the implication of what his words, and more, his actions meant. I slid my hands up his back, and he leaned forward, capturing my mouth in a slow, passionate kiss. He reached around and grabbed my ass, pulling my body closer to his, and the time apart tore through us. Finally, being reunited after over a month, all of the stress, and the doubts, and the worries dissipated. What remained was my excitement and joy, and it all poured out through our connected lips.

The feverish passion flamed quickly as our tongues swirled, and I clawed at his back. I had a store full of people, including my parents and son, yet I was tempted to test out the sturdiness of my new desk. Alec squeezed my butt one last time and pulled away. The sexy grin on his face told me he'd had the same thought.

"If we stay in here much longer, they might send out a search party."

I nodded and pressed my hand to my chest in hopes of slowing my racing heart. He waited, and when I was ready, I slipped my hand into his outstretched one and headed out. We stopped and stood just on the other side of the double steel doors. Once again, tears pricked the back of my eyes. Happiness didn't even begin to describe the emotions crashing through my being.

Alec wrapped his arms around my waist. "Baby, it's amazing.

And I'm happy to put in my application if you need a taste tester for anything."

I laughed. "Is that so?"

"I'm willing and ready to do any and everything to support you."

I tilted my head up to look at him. "You're a good man, *Chief Alec Hodge*."

"And I'm all yours."

"That you are."

Thank you for purchasing and reading! I hope you enjoyed Heat of Love. If you can spare a few more minutes of your time, I'd greatly appreciate if you'd leave a review.

If you'd like to get an extra HEA scene with Regina and Alec, you can get the bonus HERE.

Irene's story, Mechanics of Love will be out in September. Please enjoy this sneak peek.

MECHANICS OF LOVE

Madison Island thirty miles.

I sighed with relief at seeing the road sign. My two-day road trip from New York to home was nearing an end. When I'd packed my bags after the last fight with Derrick I'd only intended to stay at a hotel for a few days. I'd needed a break. We'd needed a break. Some time apart to re-evaluate our situation. But when he'd not even called looking for me after the first night... I tightened my grip on the wood grain steering wheel and mentally forced any tears to stay put.

I'd had to call him. *"Come home and stop with the dramatics."* His condescending voice taunted me. Whenever I'd called him on his bullshit, I was always being dramatic. Blowing things out of proportion. It was always me. But not this time. Not when he'd parade—I shook my head and sat up straighter in the plush leather seat of my Audi. As I settled back, I laughed quietly to myself over the fact I'd taken the car he loved the most. Was it petty? Sure. But it was purchased during the marriage which meant it was half mine. And it wasn't like either of us drove much in the city, but status, it was always about status.

After realizing he had zero intentions of apologizing—not that he ever did without there being a but included—I got the bug to get away farther. I longed for simpler. A place where I could almost remove the mask and relax just a little bit more. *Almost.*

I leaned against the headrest and daydreamed about what being myself would even look like. Hell did I even know? I'd been the reflected version of who everyone expected me to be for so long—a large branch laying across the road came into view. I yanked the steering wheel to the side, but not quickly enough to avoid it completely. My low sitting car ran over it, tossing me upwards like I'd gone over a speed bump too fast, and a cloud of dust bellowed up from the side as the sound of my tires on the dirt shoulder squealed in my ears.

The back end fishtailed before I managed to come to a screeching halt. I placed my hand over my rapidly beating heart and glanced in my rearview at the limb now shattered into pieces. Sure, this stretch of road was basically no-man's land, but fuck, they still should have people out to clear hazards from the roadways.

After a few calming breaths, I eased back onto the road. Derrick's voice taunted me, he'd have something to say about me not paying attention and somehow the branch being in the road would have been my fault. I blew out a long exhale and did a full body shake to get rid of the remaining nerves and negative thoughts about my soon-to-be-ex-husband. Sitting up, and rolling my shoulders back, I attempted to give eagle eye attention to the road ahead just in case any of the beautiful mossy oaks decided to lose more pieces.

I pushed down on the pedal, forcing the car faster, only instead of accelerating as it should have, the fine piece of German engineering—as the salesperson had called it—sputtered most unceremoniously and the dials on the dash went haywire.

"What the hell?" I pressed the gas again, the engine tried to rev in response, but again it came out more of a sputter as it jerked forward. "Great. Just fucking great." I managed to maneuver the car to the narrow shoulder.

"Now what?" I turned it off then cranked it up again. It started, but when I pressed the gas, even knowing nothing about cars, I knew the sound it made wasn't a good one.

"Damn it!" I muttered as I hit the service link button and waited for it to connect. Why couldn't I even take time away in peace without shit falling apart around me?

"Good afternoon, Mrs. Moore, how can I be of service today?" The female voice spoke over the speaker.

"Yes, the car won't go. It makes some weird noise, I think I might need a tow."

"Were you in an accident?"

"No, it just stopped."

"Are you in a safe area?"

"I'm in the middle of nowhere for the most part, but yeah, I'm fairly safe."

"Okay. One moment."

There was silence for a while, but I could hear the faint sounds of clicking as the agent worked.

"Thank you for your patience, Mrs. Moore. I have contacted the closest wrecker service. They say the estimated time to get you will be 20-30 minutes. Is that acceptable?"

I rolled my eyes, not that she could see. What option did I have? Not like if I said no, they could somehow make the driver time warp speed or something. I relayed my acceptance and declined her offer to stay on the line with me until they arrived. The time alone would give me a chance to make sure my answers to the inevitable questions were in place and delivered with practiced ease.

I hadn't told anyone I was coming for a visit. It had been a minor inconvenience with the office for me to take a sudden vacation, but I'd covered for Dr. Joyce more than once over the years, especially with his stints in rehab. He owed me. Besides, it was only two weeks. Maybe. Regardless, I knew there would be questions. From my parents, and especially from my girls. Regina and Cynthia were a lot easier to dodge virtually, too much time around them and I knew they'd start to see through, though maybe that wasn't such a bad thing.

I was tired...

My phone dinged indicating I had a new text message. I pressed the button on my steering wheel then commanded it to be read: *You need to be home by 5 today. We have dinner plans.*

The robotic voice fit the tone of my husband perfectly. We hadn't talked since he called to tell me he'd gotten my "ridiculous papers", but now he expected me to just show back up and pretend as if everything was okay. I'd served him divorce papers and he wanted to act as if it was simply a tantrum. I sighed and rested my head back against the headrest. Of course he did, because pretending all was well was what I excelled at. He'd be pissed when he found out I wasn't going to be there to play the role of the dutiful wife. That particular role was over for me.

The car continued to make an awful noise as it ran, but I needed to keep the AC going. April in coastal Georgia meant high humidity and I'd be sweating all too soon and I did not need my edges curling up. Besides, the only time one was permitted to perspire was when working out, but even then, one glistened, they didn't sweat. At least according to my mother.

The sound of a big engine got my attention. I sat up and squinted at the sight of an approaching vehicle. As it got closer, I could tell it was the tow I'd been waiting for, though I expected to see it coming in my rearview, not in front of me. There was absolutely nothing along this stretch of road from the direction the truck came other than Madison Island. I turned off my car then stepped out as the driver stopped and did a U-turn in the middle of the two-lane road so they could back up in front of my broken-down vehicle. The logo on the door pulled a deep groan from my throat. *Martin Autobody.*

All the talk from Cynthia and Regina about how my high school nemesis, Remi, now ran her father's mechanic shop and worked wonders on their cars ping ponged through my head. Not to mention Remi had been instrumental in getting Regina's food truck which was doing well along with the storefront. Somehow the woman who'd never been a part of my friend circle seemed to have wormed her way in and I wasn't sure how I felt about it.

I had the momentary thought it might not be her in the truck, but was quickly proven wrong when the driver hopped down. It'd been over twenty years since Remi Martin and I had said much to each other. Sure, I'd see her in passing around town when I was home for visits, but we'd never done the whole catch-up thing. There wasn't any need. But here she was, in a set of dirty blue overalls with the top half tied around her waist and a black T-shirt with the unfortunate nickname clinging to a figure I never knew she had. Oversized, baggy clothes had always been her go-to.

She'd also fully embraced the tomboy look where her hair was concerned. Wasn't quite the total low cut with line-up, because she did have tight curls on top, though I'd have to say Derrick probably sported more hair than she did. And I was sure he probably spent way more time on his. Being well groomed was all part of his façade.

When she laid eyes on me, she laughed and shook her head. "Irene Johnson."

I didn't bother to correct her by adding the Moore to my name. "Nice to see you too, Remi."

She drew together what were surprisingly well shaped brows. "Is it?"

"Isn't that the typical greeting when you see someone you've not been around in a while?"

"Only if you mean it, otherwise why lie?"

Just like in high school. Blunt without a care of how her words came across. Was it really that hard to pretend? To put forth basic politeness? The multitude of fake smiles and air kiss greetings I'd perfected, given, and received over the years flipped through my head.

As she turned her attention to my car, appraising it with open appreciation, clearly for her the answer was yes. She whistled through her teeth. "The Audi TT RS with a two-point five-liter turbocharged engine giving it three hundred ninety-four horsepower. Zero to sixty in three point six seconds." She moved around the side to the back. "Oh, the sport exhaust. I bet it sounds like a beast on the road. It's...a...beauty. What's wrong with it?"

I didn't have a clue about most of what she'd rattled off. I did however pick up on the fact she was impressed and on reflex that made me stand a little bit taller. "How am I supposed to know? It was going then it wasn't."

She rounded the car, easing past me as she continued to check it out. "Did you run out of gas?"

I planted both hands on my hips and frowned at her. "Did you just ask me if I ran out of gas? Is that the mechanic equivalent of did you power it on?"

She lifted one shoulder, but didn't answer. Instead, she tilted her head and simply stared at me waiting.

"No, I didn't run out of gas. Aren't you just here to tow it to a certified place, not play diagnostic on the side of the road?"

"Crank it up," she ordered, completely ignoring what I'd said.

It'd irked me to no end when she'd do that in high school. She'd either pretend I hadn't said something, or act unbothered by my words. Other people cared about what I'd had to say, and what my opinion of them was. Everyone but Remi Martin.

"No. Look, I know Regina and Cynthia sing your praises, but really there is nothing you can do for me here other than put it on your truck and take it to a service location."

I was annoyed enough that the damn car died on me. She wasn't helping by keeping me out longer than needed by trying to do something I was fairly certain she wasn't qualified for. I didn't know much about cars, but I did remember how much

Derrick talked about certified this and certified that. I drove, he handled everything else, or rather would call for the concierge service to come take care of it whenever work was needed.

"Suit yourself." Remi headed back to her truck, pulled a lever, and after a squeak, and a thud, the back slowly began lowering to the ground. She went about dragging chains toward my car then dropped to her knees to peer under it. "Did you run over something?"

I pushed my sunglasses up to the top of my head. "For goodness sakes, Remi, stop with all the damn questions."

She laughed again which only served to annoy me more, then flipped onto her back, not caring one bit about laying in the dirt to attach the chains to my car. The muscles in her arms flexed and tensed while she worked. I inched forward to squat down, placing my palm on the side of the vehicle to help with my balance, in an attempt to get a closer look.

She sat up, brushing against me in the process which nearly knocked me backwards. With quick reflexes she caught my arm to keep me from busting my ass. Her grip was firm and hot, and I wasn't sure which stunned me more, her touching me, or my near fall.

She pulled us both to standing. "You good?" I nodded and only then did she release me. She dusted off her hands. "You're leaking fluid, so you may have punctured something. Hence why I asked if you ran over something."

Her quick swerve right back to business jolted me out of my odd stupor and I wiped at the spot on my forearm which now sported an abstract dirty handprint. Without waiting for me to reply, she went back to her truck and my car lurched forward before it was slowly pulled onto the flat bed. I watched it, instead of giving too much attention to the woman with me.

"A tree branch."

"What?"

"A little ways back, there was a tree branch in the road."

"Why didn't you drive around it?"

"Why is that any of your concern?" I shot back.

She shook her head and headed for the driver's side of her truck. "Go around and hop in."

"Hop in what?"

She looked at the cab of her vehicle then climbed in. She couldn't be serious.

Pre-Order Available. Coming September 22

ABOUT THE AUTHOR

Meka James is a writer of adult contemporary and erotic romance. A born and raised Georgia Peach, she still resides in the southern state with her hubby of 16 years and counting. Mom to four kids of the two legged variety, she also has four fur-babies of the canine variety. Leo the turtle and Spade the snake rounds out her wacky household. When not writing or reading, Meka can be found playing The Sims 3, sometimes Sims 4, and making up fun stories to go with the pixelated people whose world she controls.

https://www.authormekajames.com/

OTHER BOOKS BY MEKA

Fiendish: A Twisted Fairytale

please note this book tackles dark themes that may be upsetting to readers. You don't have to read Fiendish to read and enjoy Not Broken

Not Broken: The Happily Ever After

*Continuation of Calida's story from Fiendish

The Lists

*Extended HEA for Calida and Malcolm from Not Broken

Anything Once

*Erotic romance featuring Ian and Quinn Faraday who are on a journey to spice up their sex lives

Desert Rose Hook-ups series

Being Neighborly

Being Hospitable

Being Cordial